Praise for

Mask

"…a very unique twist to storytelling."

—Dark Diva Reviews

Wylde

"With a dash of humor, some sensual lovemaking scenes and a mystery to solve, Wylde is definitely a story you don't want to miss."

—Literary Nymphs

The Hired Man

"It stands apart in the M/M genre with characters that aren't conventional, yet manage to work their way into your heart."

—Whipped Cream Erotic Romance Reviews

The Pleasure Slave

"…her two main characters pop from the pages of this story."

—Book Wenches

http://www.dreamspinnerpress.com

Books by
JAN IRVING

The Hired Man
Mask
Mastering Toby
Wylde

ebooks by
JAN IRVING

The Pleasure Slave
The Star Man
The Summer Gardener

All published by
DREAMSPINNER PRESS

Mastering Toby

Jan Irving

Dreamspinner Press

Published by
Dreamspinner Press
4760 Preston Road
Suite 244-149
Frisco, TX 75034
http://www.dreamspinnerpress.com/

Mastering Toby

Cover Art by Paul Richmond http://www.paulrichmondstudio.com

ISBN: 978-1-61581-364-3

Printed in the United States of America
First Edition
March, 2010

eBook edition available
eBook ISBN: 978-1-61581-365-0

For Paul Richmond with thanks
for creating such beautiful covers for me.

And for Cindy, who loved Sahara Blue.

And thanks to the wonderful Lyn Gala,
who read every chapter and lit my way.

Like the moon, come out from behind the clouds. Shine!

—Buddha

Chapter 1

TOBY RAFFERTY was sitting on his ass in a closet of his condo. Just outside the yellow outline of the door, he could clearly make out the sounds of his twenty-fifth birthday party rolling like film destined for the can.

He was peeling the label off his Bud. He paused and took a sip, thinking maybe it was good to feel nothing. Not pain, not despair. The man he felt locked tight inside him, like a butterfly caught in barbed wire.

The door creaked and he squinted up into the light, knowing who would be there before he saw the leather sandals, the muscled chest, and abdomen. The man had a dragon tat snaking across flesh he knew about as intimately as he did the flesh of any of Jared Asche's lovers. Well, they *were* lovers: lovers on the for-cable gay soap called *Mission Bay*, set in San Diego.

"Toby." The gentle voice and a hand ruffled his hair, and then Jared shoved some of Toby's winter coats aside so he could slouch on the opposite side of the closet.

Jared had dark hair falling over his forehead, warm brown eyes, a strange tan color that was sometimes soft as toffee, sometimes hot and sizzling like butter in the pan, depending on the scene, the mood Jared channeled. Now he was his typical Zen self, giving off Buddha vibes as he sat unshaven, his shirt open, wearing purple shorts with surfers displayed. His beach bum look suited him since he lived in a floating house tied to a wharf a mile from Toby's condo.

Toby shoved his blond mussed hair out of his eyes, shrugging. "A fucking *lot* of people, you know?" All her friends, friends of his girlfriend Anita's since Toby didn't really have any friends, except for Jared and maybe Ellen the makeup artist. She was always showing him her tag sale finds. It made him feel worse, somehow, all these people here who were really Allison's, and it was his birthday.

"I do know." Jared reached out and cupped Toby's head, leaning so his forehead brushed Toby's. Jesus! No wonder their fans were sure they were lovers for real, Toby reflected, and not for the first time. He stifled a sad laugh.

As if he'd ever have the courage to—

He cut off the thought before he could finish it.

But he was comfortable with Jared, never mind Jared was gay and Toby was straight. That had been a bone of contention with his stepfather when he'd stuck with quiet stubbornness to this friendship. They had been best friends since their excruciatingly embarrassing first love scene on the show for the episode called "Awakening."

Toby took another pull of his beer, thinking again not for the first time that the title of that ep had been meaningful, though he hadn't seen it at the time.

"Want to go to my place?" He arched a dark brow, giving Toby a mild look. Jared had the perfect hook, hanging easy in the water, resting just at the surface so that Toby couldn't help but bite. It was almost like Jared had set out to tune into a wavelength just for Toby.

"I really shouldn't. You know Anita went to a lot of trouble...." Toby's voice drifted off. He wanted to go. They both knew it.

"For her friends, yeah." With a wicked curl to the lips and for the first time that night, Toby laughed. It felt good, almost alien, and then familiar sadness took away the moment like breath took the light from a candle.

"Toby True Heart," Jared teased. Jared was thirty, assured, and a mandolin musician when he had time away from shooting. Toby admired him. He was so comfortable with himself, even remaining calm when Toby's homophobic stepfather tried to bait him. "What am I going to do with you, dude?"

For some reason that made heat rise in Toby's cheeks, and he remembered how often when he came over to Jared's place his co-star's bed was rumpled and one of his "dates" was lying around, watching TV or eating cereal. Jared was nothing like Toby, who had only ever been with one person his whole life—his high school sweetheart, Anita.

But lately he caught himself looking at those boyfriends of Jared's, at their relaxed, smiling faces, at the way Jared liked to spoil them, cooking for them, lightly running a hand over their arms, teasing them, and he wondered what it would be like to be one of them. To stay over with Jared.

"You're so adorable."

"Fuck you." Toby pulled his knees up, finding one of his legs had lost circulation; somehow he wobbled to his feet, but when he nearly took a spill, Jared made a rough sound and gave the offending leg a brisk rub, always taking care in that way he had about him, as if Toby somehow belonged to him and he had to look out for him.

Looking at the lean, deft brown hands, one of his wrists ringed by a turquoise hoop, Toby experienced that strange tight feeling in his gut. It happened more and more often. Weird. Maybe it was a by-product of playing a gay character. Well, his stepfather had warned him that it might rub off, the whole gay thing. In fact, he went so far as to say Toby must have a secret if he took a role on the soap.

Alas, Toby had no secrets. He was safe and boring, but he ached inside. He wished he could just figure out what for; it was like he'd spent his whole life on the verge of becoming… what? He swallowed thickly. "I want to get a little baked, okay?" He could let it go with Jared. Jared would keep him safe, and with Jared, the ache went away, smoothed out.

Jared's eyes were sober as he studied Toby. "Yeah, okay. Come on."

JARED watched as Toby kissed his blond, tanned Barbie doll of a girlfriend, Anita, snuggling her from behind. She had sleek, shapely arms and perfect skin that set off her green eyes.

Bitch.

He closed his eyes, taking a deep breath. Man, he had to keep a lid on his feelings, because he was in danger of behaving like the stereotypical fag in love with his best friend, resentful of the proof he was straight. But he didn't think that she was good for Toby, not at all, stamping all over Toby's puppy feelings with stiletto ruthlessness.

He also acknowledged that he was somewhat biased, because he was in love with Toby.

He had been from the first moment they'd met, sipping sodas while they outlined their debut erotic scene with input from the director and the writers. He had seen right away Toby was innocent, that he had very little clue about anything but the most vanilla sex in general, never mind sex with another man. His blue eyes, sun-streaked hair, and silky muscled form rang Jared's bell, but Toby also aroused protective feelings. So Jared had shoved the sexual heat aside as much as he could and acted an older brother to Toby.

An older brother who had to maintain a handle on his feelings to keep himself from giving Toby more than he'd ever ask for, such as a burning kiss on the mouth.

Jared inhaled, concentrating on his breathing as he did in daily meditation. It didn't take away the feeling, but it did keep him centered.

A wisp of thought crossed his mind, not for the first time as he watched Toby with his girlfriend. Why had Toby taken the role on *Mission Bay* in the first place? It seemed a strange choice for a shy, straight boy-next-door type.

And why did Jared's instincts always whisper there was more to him?

"But will you stay there overnight like last time?" Anita prodded.

Yes, bitch, in my bed. Your boyfriend spread out, open, taking my cock, grabbing my ass as I—

But then Anita continued, and Jared couldn't quite hate her.

"I mean, Toby...." Her gaze flashed to Jared and she lowered her voice. "Just make sure your stepdad doesn't find out, okay? I know you guys are only friends but... awkward! And I don't want to referee again."

Jared took another deep breath, closing out the fantasy that had run through his head as he held Anita's aware green eyes. She knew that Jared was in love with her boyfriend. Didn't she think Jared was any kind of threat?

He swallowed the burning feeling in his throat, wanting to hate her just for that.

When Toby kissed her, Jared had to turn away from seeing Toby pleading with those soft lips to be allowed off the leash for one night.

Jesus! There was only so much he could take. He wanted to be the one Toby looked to for approval, for permission. And the lover in him wanted to master innocent Toby, to conquer him in bed and leave him sweaty and smiling.

Yeah, right. Like that would ever happen. The most he could have was to be Toby's loyal best friend.

TOBY climbed into Jared's baby blue vintage DeSoto after running a hand over the fins in a friendly way. He smiled at Jared, noticing some faint tension around his friend's mouth. Maybe it was Anita. She was carefully neutral about Jared for some reason, but Toby had refused against all odds to give up his friendship, so she stayed out of it when he'd argued with his family about his choice of friend.

Jared was nurturing. There was something about him, sure of himself, protective, so that Toby felt better after spending some time around him. It wasn't that he made Toby feel uncertain, like he needed to lean, the way he reluctantly had to admit he'd fallen into the habit of doing sometimes with Anita while navigating their familiar mine field. Instead, Toby conversely felt stronger around Jared, more himself.

It popped into his head not for the first time that Jared must be an amazing lover. Giving, in control, completely focused on whoever was in his bed.

Toby rubbed his forehead, thinking it was late; he was depressed and a little needy. But he hoped that they could spend some time alone, that none of Jared's lovers were around.

He wanted him all to himself.

AT THE wharf, Jared swung the car into his parking space and looked over at a sleepy Toby. Fuck, he looked adorable, hair combed by the wind, trusting gaze on Jared. It was all he could do not to lean close and kiss those lips. He did it on the show all the time, of course, so he knew how Toby tasted, but he wanted Toby for real.

Grimacing over the sudden tightness in his shorts, he opened the door and waited for Toby to follow him, putting an arm with casual possessiveness around his friend's shoulders as they headed for his houseboat. He didn't imagine the way Toby leaned against him, almost like they were more than friends; it made his heart pick up.

Mixed signals. Shit.

"Will Tom be there, do you think?" Toby asked, big blue eyes exploring Jared's face.

"Huh, don't think so. He went on a fishing trip." Jared shrugged. He couldn't think of anyone else when he was with Toby, but he wondered why Toby had asked about the other man. In his fantasy world, it was a sign of Toby's jealousy.

"Right." Toby's warmth ghosted against Jared's skin, making Jared want to pull him closer. He struggled with his dominant side, the part that latched onto Toby's receptiveness. He didn't want to think about Toby's sex life with Anita, but if he was her, he'd tie the other man to a bed and then....

Whoa. Jared's eyes widened. Now he was imagining himself in her place just so he could touch the man he loved? Clearly he needed to get away for a while again and regain his perspective.

"What about Malcolm?"

Jared blinked. "I think he's in Florida right now," he said, letting his arm fall as they reached the glass and deck structure of his boathouse, rocking minutely in moorage. It had two levels with a flat roof up top for barbeques and a place to grow herbs. Jared kept it ruthlessly organized since the space was so tight. If he bought something new, something old had to go, but that was okay since he recycled religiously. "Why do you want to know what the guys are up to?" He cocked a brow at Toby.

Toby shrugged, innocent blue eyes holding Jared's. "Don't want to intrude."

"I invited you. I want you here." Jared gave Toby a level glance as he unlocked his front door. It had herons etched over the glass— easily breakable for a burglar, but the inset was something special he was reluctant to replace, despite the cautious lectures of his friend Sahara Blue Drummond, who was an ex Navy SEAL and now worked part time at a local security company. Jared didn't have much of value anyway, other than his mandolins and some of his finer hand-made toys.

"Yeah, but—" Toby looked a little embarrassed. This was intriguing. What *was* going through his mind?

"But what? We'll smoke a little grass, watch an action movie. Perfect for your birthday, right?" Jared checked the contents in his fridge, pulling out the brand of beer he kept just for Toby. Shit, he had it bad, if he was supplying favorite beverages.

Toby had settled on Jared's green velvet couch, wrapping the thin Kelim rug Jared had picked up on a trip to Turkey around himself as usual, as if he were cold or lost. It never failed to touch Jared, so he wanted to stand and stare at Toby's giving pink lips and tanned healthy skin, skin which was silky to the touch of his callused musician's fingers. Jared wanted to reach out and smooth away whatever the unhappiness was he sensed in Toby.

"I just thought you might want to be with someone," Toby said.

"I am." Jared said, handing him his beer. "With someone."

"You know what I mean. Someone you spend time with."

"Someone I fuck." Jared took a deep pull from his own bottle. Just saying that word aloud to Toby made all kinds of images rise like resurrected ghosts.

"Yeah, that wouldn't be me." Toby took another swallow and kept his gaze on his feet.

Oh man. He couldn't say anything, since if he did, it would be the truth: that Jared wanted to start on Toby's feet, kissing, licking the sensitive spaces between his toes. He could have Toby hard and begging—

He turned away, reminding himself that however attractive he found Toby, however much the submissive signals caught his attention like a pale fish flashing in the murk of the ocean when he snorkeled, Toby was not gay. Not unless he said so and made it damn obvious, anyway.

Jared snorted to himself, searching through a campy tiki chest for some of his supply. "Chuck Norris tonight?" he asked, thinking maybe Chuck would get his mind off his unrequited passion.

"Huh. Something early, like seventies?"

"Lusty chest hair Chuck. Right." Jared located his stash and slumped on his couch next to the delicious and unobtainable Toby. Toby still looked worried, no doubt anxious he'd somehow offended Jared, so Jared smiled at him, quirking a brow. "Dude, will you relax? I'll make cupcakes and put a candle on one of them if you need the Hallmark moment."

"Ha ha, okay." Toby dropped his head forward, shoulders hunched.

Jared stopped rolling their treat for a second and rubbed one of Toby's shoulders in absent comfort, not thinking anything of it until Toby caught his breath.

He looked up sharply. Something was off. Something different?

Toby colored and winced when Jared repeated the motion.

"Dude?" Jared asked.

"I pulled a muscle or something," Toby mumbled.

Off, definitely something off. Jared opened his mouth, but Toby leaned forward and kissed him.

What the fuck!

"What did you do *that* for?" Jared growled, shaken hard.

"I—" Toby rubbed his faint beard shadow. "Just telling you I appreciate how you look out for me. It seemed natural."

"No, it's not, Toby."

"I'm sorry." Toby had a hand over his face, looking miserably embarrassed.

Jared ached for him, but this was his line in the sand. Casual touching, okay, they both seemed to do that, had done that from the beginning, hands all over each other. Jared seemed to be the only one who saw the subtext there, but casual "friendly" kissing? Fuck being polite, he couldn't take that. He'd shove his tongue in Toby's mouth and scare him, fuck up their friendship.

"We do it all the time on the show," Toby said.

"That's not real." And that kiss, the brush of Toby's warm silky lips against his own, so that he sung with sensory memory—that was all too real to Jared. As real as the boner he crossed a leg to conceal. "I can't kiss you as a friend, all right?"

"Of course, I don't know what I was thinking! Jesus, it's not like I kiss my other guy friends." Toby shook his head.

"Thanks, I think." Jared shook his head, completely exasperated. Did Toby not take him seriously as a man? He was just a familiar piece of comfy furniture? Fuck! "But I'm a gay man, so something like that could qualify as teasing," he admitted, his eyes not meeting Toby's.

Toby gave a ragged sigh. "Shit! I don't know what I was thinking. You're my good thing, Jared. I'm sorry I overstepped."

How to handle this? Toby was his, no matter the fantasies he set off with every unconscious movement. But if he couldn't have him in his bed, under him, he wanted to take care of Toby the only way he could, as his protective older friend.

"You idiot. You get a free pass since it's your birthday but just don't kiss me again." Jared swallowed a healthy amount of his beer as he dug out the DVD of the movie they'd watch. What he wanted to add but didn't was, *don't kiss me unless you mean it.*

Chapter 2

AT FIRST Toby was reticent, especially since Jared had touched the
bruise. Fuck! He didn't want even Jared to know about that; he'd
totally misunderstand. He was glad that it was late and they were
drinking and smoking weed so Jared wouldn't suggest they shuck their
clothes and go swimming, something they did together occasionally
when he came over to Jared's amazing houseboat.

Jared had some crab traps that he liked to check some nights.
Toby couldn't stand shellfish, and crabs freaked him out, looking like
spiders crawling around underwater, but Jared never teased him about
it, and Toby appreciated that. It was just one more way his friend was a
positive person in his life, unlike his only other male role model,
Toby's stepfather. Mike Danvers had made it clear from day one when
he'd married Toby's Mom that he found Toby wanting, a klutz at
playing football, not great at math or sciences and therefore not bound
for university; more a dreamer who liked to drift, who was agreeable to
everyone's plans.

Living under his roof, Toby had huddled more and more into
himself growing up. He liked to dabble with art sometimes or write
poetry. He liked to imagine himself living a different life, which had
led to a secret enjoyment of taking drama in high school.

He knew if he exposed himself, who he really was, his confidence
would be chipped away, his ideas questioned, and by the time he left
high school, Toby didn't have much confidence. But he did have Anita,
who was his center. She was so much more glamorous than he was, so
much more a driven achiever, full of fire. Sometimes Toby was sure

she was a piece of the puzzle of what he wanted—that her drive was something he himself needed to emulate. If he could only figure out what he wanted so he could fight for it.

So he wasn't the most ambitious guy. He wouldn't even have auditioned for the role he'd won on the soap if the guy he was cleaning pools for hadn't thought he looked perfect for the role. He was connected, so Toby fell into his chance.

This was a real job, his first, but he couldn't talk about it much with his family. "Fucking porn for queers," his stepfather had called it, dismissing Toby's show at Sunday dinner when he'd confessed he'd taken the role. "Jesus, I hope no one recognizes you!"

His girlfriend remained neutral about it, and he'd been grateful for that since his family was so pissed, though she'd gotten a bit testy when he'd started spending so much time with Jared.

But the bruise on his back was worth it.

Some time into the movie, Toby noticed Jared had fallen asleep, his dark hair falling over his forehead, his face scrunched against a tangerine silk pillow from one of his travels. Toby hated it when Jared went away, like when he went on the trip to Morocco last fall. He'd missed him so much.

Fucking pathetic.

Seeing Jared was safely asleep and wouldn't get mad if Toby got too close, Toby curled against Jared's larger body, staring up at the ceiling and the wavering light, relaxing only when Jared put an arm around him.

SOMETHING was wrong. Jared felt it before his eyes flared open. Another body was mashed against his, and he never slept like this, plastered against anyone. The only person he could remotely imagine wanting to do it with was—

Toby.

Cool air against his body now. Toby had pulled away from him.

Jared rubbed his eyes, groggy, still relaxed from the grass, his penis hard from Toby's proximity. "Hey," he rasped.

Toby was bent forward, face averted. He gave a shaky laugh.

Frowning in concern now, Jared leaned forward and gently touched his shoulder, not wanting to hurt him if it was sore for some reason. "Toby, man."

Toby flashed a look at him and Jared glimpsed the bleak suffering in his eyes, as if he was fighting tears. What the fuck!

As Jared watched, grappling for the right thing to say, to ask, Toby stared out the floor-to-ceiling windows running along Jared's great room, looking out at the small bay where lights dotted the water like blurry oil blobs. The moon was reflected in a bright path on the wavy surface, softened by cloud, yet bright enough to reveal Toby scrubbing his eyes.

Every part of him wanted to bark out a command to know what was going on with Toby. Half-awake, half-baked, Jared struggled to master his anger. *Someone had hurt Toby.*

He shifted closer instinctively, keeping his movements easy, noticing that nevertheless Toby tensed, watching him out of the corner of his eye. Fuck it! He pulled Toby into his arms. His throat burned with a need to ask; he'd glimpsed shame and confusion in Toby's blue eyes.

"Do you ever wonder where you belong, what you should be doing with your life?" Toby asked. "I know everyone thinks I'm so easy going, but I think about it all the time. I feel like I'm traveling in the wrong direction like that horoscope deal you talked about."

Throat tight out of concern for Toby, Jared nevertheless smiled a little. "Mercury retrograde, right. It's when Mercury the messenger appears to travel backward; it's attributed to causing all kinds of problems with people communicating."

"I feel that way all the time, man." Toby rubbed a hand through his hair in frustration. "What am I doing wrong? When I go along with people, they chip away at the things that make me happy but when I let myself think about other shit…. Scary, you know?"

"It's okay, baby. I get scared, too, all the time." Jared traced circles of comfort over Toby's back, not caring that he was hard and that Toby had to feel it. Right now it mattered more to give solace for the wound he didn't understand but could feel in Toby.

"You don't seem scared. You seem so strong, even with the shit said about you sometimes for being gay." Toby's face crumpled. He turned toward Jared, hands clenching in his muscled shoulders, holding on. He whispered, "I'm sorry."

Jared answered, absolutely honest, "You don't need to be anything for me, Tobes. You don't have to say the right thing or do the right thing. Not with me."

Toby stared at him. The two of them were tangled together like flotsam washed up on a beach after a storm. "Oh God, Jared, you would say something like that!" He gave another odd little laugh before leaning forward and placing his lips against Jared's.

Sudden lightning zapped through Jared's body. Like a tree on the verge of falling, like a wave about to hit the beach, he trembled, but it was no contest, no fucking contest. He'd pushed Toby away before, drawn the line but now Toby was stepping over it.

He yanked him closer. Was that rough sound of need coming from Toby or from himself? He didn't know as he feasted on Toby's mouth, penetrating him, growling at the perfect feel of some part of him inside of Toby while Toby's hands kneaded his shoulders and he tried to kiss Jared back. Awkwardly.

Oh Christ! Toby didn't seem to have much experience, and that lit Jared up, lit him like the grogginess and the need to press himself, to press his erection between Toby's legs, and he knew he shouldn't do this, not now, there was something—

Toby fell back and let him, let him. He made a cradle for Jared's larger body, and when his strong legs wrapped around Jared's hips, embracing Jared… that was it! That was fucking it!

He rubbed against Toby, feeling himself sliding against something hard. Toby was hard?

Jared took Toby's wrists and pinned them above his head, holding startled blue eyes. "I need…." Christ, he was almost incoherent! No time to explain he needed some part of Toby anchored, held down. For him, for Toby—it was all instinct, like a wolf mounting his mate.

"Love you, Tobes," he mumbled, on the verge. Oh God, he never thought he'd be this close to Toby for real! Thrusting, thrusting faster now, squeezing his eyes tightly shut. "Love you so much."

"I know," Toby whispered, softly, sadly, nuzzling his face against Jared's. He was compliant—something was not quite right about it, but Jared's body took it for the surrender he craved. His neck corded and his toes curled and his body roared satisfaction as he came, rubbing himself off on Toby, wishing his cock was free and Toby was naked so he could see his come spatter silky skin.

Marking Toby his.

Heart pounding, head pounding, sweaty, shocky, staring into a pair of dazed blue eyes, eyes weighted by secrets and had Toby even come? Oh Jesus. Shaking, Jared opened his mouth to ask—

And then Toby's BlackBerry purred, and he sat up, rubbing against Jared's wildly sensitive lower body, making him shudder spasmodically. There was no time to recover or to think. He could feel the warm wet spot between them chill as Toby reached into his front pocket and shifted away from Jared, turning his back, answering his call. And who else could it be but *her*?

"Hey, baby," Toby said, rubbing a hand through his hair, hunched over.

Jared jolted off the couch, his usual grace gone, and he almost tripped over the fallen Kelim. Toby looked up at him, staring.

He staggered through the hallway into his small bathroom, trembling, cold now—and he was always so together, so calm, and that was what Toby said he loved about him.

He flung open the john and heaved up the grass, the sudden upset twisting his guts, his eyes spilling tears.

When he caught his breath, Jared was able to climb to his feet. He removed his wet clothing, not looking at it as he cannoned it into the hamper, not meeting his own gaze in the mirror.

Oh shit! He'd told Toby that he—

Warm water. Hot. He turned it on full blast, knowing that on his houseboat the spray wouldn't last that long, but he needed it, because he was cold to the bones. He got in under the water and wrapped his arms around himself, still shaking.

Destroyed and remade by Toby.

TOBY huddled on the couch, back stiff as if anticipating a blow, waiting.

He heard the shower start, listened to the spray drum, and wished he could be in there with Jared, washed clean. After what seemed like an aching stretch of forever, he heard the water shut off. He stiffened when the bathroom door opened and warmth and steam invaded the colder great room.

But then he heard Jared's bedroom door quietly close.

Toby put his head in his hands. What a loser he was!

Wrapping the Kelim around himself, he climbed to his feet, drifting closer to Jared's alluring, forbidden, and terrifying bedroom door. He grazed the silent wood with his hand before sliding down to the floor, huddling outside Jared's door as he had a few hours ago in the safety of a closet.

THE sun slanted in low like a hot spotlight, rippling off the water and hitting the ceiling in waving patterns to wake Toby. He scrubbed his eyes, experiencing that peaceful feeling he'd had as a kid when he'd woken up over the summer holidays. Maybe the only thing he needed to do was cut the grass today for the old man.

Then his eyes flared open as he remembered last night. He sat up, heart pounding. Jared's bedroom door was open, his room abandoned, the statue of Kwan Yin at his meditation altar sparkling as the pasted fake jewels in her hair caught fire.

Jared was gone; he must have stepped over Toby, left him sleeping.

Knowing he wasn't going to find the answer to the heavy ache in his chest but nevertheless needing to see that for himself, Toby got up and walked slowly to the open galley kitchen. He caught the scent of espresso, and when he touched the coffee pot, it was still warm.

He knew where Jared kept his mugs, so Toby reached for one and a note fell out. Jared must have known this was the first thing Toby would do; he knew Toby so well.

The bread's iffy, but there's fresh fruit in the fridge—J.

Toby swallowed thickly, filling his coffee mug, hands clenched around the fragment of warmth from Jared's care. He couldn't eat, not right now, not feeling like everything was fucked up between them. He'd only meant to please Jared; Anita kept hinting that he was in love with Toby.

Toby laughed bitterly. Had he done that, kissed Jared, allowed him to work himself off against Toby's compliant body merely to give back to him, to seduce him into never deserting Toby?

Taking his coffee and returning to Jared's room, as if he could still have the conversation he both craved and dreaded, he sat down on Jared's freshly made bed. As he scrubbed his hair off his forehead, bleak amusement moved through his chest; Jared had made the bed, neat and orderly even after the disaster of what had happened between them, even though last night he'd seemed upset, his shocked brown eyes holding Toby's as Toby took his call from Anita.

Moved to reach out, needing to somehow make this better—but how did he make this better? Shit!—Toby put the coffee aside and circled the room, searching for something that would give him an opening, a way to reach Jared, to make him still want Toby. He opened drawers, cheeks heating because this was something he'd never done at home and only taken up while living with Anita to get a clue to her mood, her intentions.

But Toby hit jackpot at the last drawer in Jared's dark-stained minimal bamboo dresser, next to his altar. Under the spill of rose quartz worry beads was a tidy nest of paraphernalia. Toby was not really sure what exactly he was looking at first, maybe just some way to reach Jared, something that he could use as leverage. He pulled out a bulbous form, blown glass with scarlet streams, cool and sensuously curved in his hand, the feel of it stirring him for some inexplicable reason; then his eyes widened as he recognized the shape of an erect penis.

He rubbed the cool glass against his bottom lip, closing his eyes. Okay, this was it, his way to connect with Jared, make up for what had happened.

If he had the courage to use it.

Chapter 3

THE next day at the studio after they finished shooting, Toby approached Jared. "I borrowed something from your place," he confessed, swallowing as he looked into Jared's eyes for the first time since the weekend. Silently, with an odd kind of ceremony, he offered him an oblong box.

Jared stared at him, roused from brooding. They were almost ready to go over the blocking, using two cameras to capture a conversation between his character, Aspen, and his lover Kelly, played by Toby. Then they'd film the segment that Jared was dreading— Aspen making love to Kelly. How could he mount Toby again and have it not feel real?

He'd relived those moments from the boat over and over again. He remembered Toby's wide startled blue eyes, remembered Toby acting as if he had no idea what he'd invited. He remembered rubbing himself, caught up completely like a seaman pulled under by a siren.

"How are you?" Inane question, but he needed to know. He kept picturing Toby slumped in the background like a wallflower at another one of Anita's frequent gatherings. Not that he could really do anything about it. Toby belonged to her.

"I miss you," Toby said, squeezing his eyes shut. "I'm sorry but I can't let this go on—you pushed me too far, Jared."

"What do you mean, Tobes?" Confused, Jared finally reached for a familiar blue gray rectangular box, conscious of the vivid lighting, of the people bustling around them. "Do you even know what this is?" he rasped, aware from the few clues he had that Toby seemed to live a very vanilla sex life. It didn't help that when he'd originally ordered it, he'd pictured using it in Toby. Christ, like that would ever happen!

For an answer, Toby reached out and removed *Intrigue,* smooth polished hardwood, a piece of undulating sculpture. "I looked it up." He held Jared's gaze though his skin was flushed, perspiring under the combination of the heat of the lights and Jared's stare. Still, Jared picked up an odd vibe coming from him, a mixture of anticipation and determination. "It's beautiful; not what I'd expected for kinky stuff, but completely what I expect from you."

"Not so loud, please," Jared ordered. "That's deeply personal. And yeah, I, uh, have a kinky side." He liked to tie men up sometimes, not that he'd ever wanted Toby to know that.

Toby's shoulders slumped as he watched Jared take the box and replace the anal stimulator, face calm, but hands shaking. "You shouldn't have borrowed this! Jesus, Toby!"

"Don't worry, I washed it." Bleak humor moved through Toby's gaze. He must have seen the way Jared's eyes widened at what his statement revealed. "Oh yes, I used it. I lubed it up and put it in me."

Christ! Jared took Toby's arm, leading him into a doorway alcove, staking out what privacy he could. He stared at him, at a loss for words. All he could see was Toby on his bed, his legs open, wanton, using Jared's smooth toy. He was moved to say exactly the wrong thing, but he couldn't help himself, "Did you enjoy it?"

"Yes." Toby scrunched his face. "But I don't think I was that good with it. Clearly I need you to tutor me."

"Toby!" Jared was having a hard time breathing. "What the fuck!"

Toby's parted lips made Jared flash back to the many times he'd seen him kiss his girlfriend, asking her permission for something. Lips he'd then pressed against Jared's, spinning his world. "I just wanted to understand you."

Jared ran a hand over the box. It aroused him that Toby had taken the toy. Fuck, he was picking up on Toby's confusion, living what Toby felt, which wasn't good for him or Toby. The second he recognized that, part of him had stepped back, was critical of his own behavior in the way of a naturally dominant man with his lover.

"I like to play with bondage." Jared cleared his throat, blushing, but Toby had been frank with him, had fucking floored him, so he was moved to reciprocate. "So, kinky, but with incense and crystals, of course."

"Of course." Toby had humor glinting in his eyes. He grazed fingers over the back of Jared's hand, and little bursts of electricity tingled through Jared's skin in response. Hushed, as if his feelings were more intimate than showing off the toy, Toby spoke. "You don't answer my calls or let me inside when I come by your place. You locked me out. Aren't we friends anymore, or did I fuck that up? I have to know, Jared."

"I can't right now, Tobes," Jared said. He swallowed thickly, thinking he should talk about why, but he couldn't; it was all wadded up inside his chest. *I love you.* Shit! How often had he castigated himself over the past long, miserable days for saying those words? He'd tried to meditate, but he couldn't concentrate on his breathing when those words, the remembered feel of Toby's surrender, haunted him. And he hadn't been able to face Toby until work had forced him out of seclusion.

"*Five minutes, Toby and Jared!*" the director's assistant called, real life breaking in, relentless, when Jared just wished he could be alone again.

"You won't let me talk to you outside of work, and I know after we do this scene you'll run away again." Toby's hand dug into Jared's arm. Jared wanted to crush him close. He felt protective, sexual. He wanted to cover Toby's body, so Toby almost couldn't breathe. It was an insane feeling he would control, like how he wanted to feed Toby his cock, his come, make Toby only taste that for an entire day.

"I'm not running away!" Jared made a chopping motion with his hand, trying to deny his fantasies. Shit! He could almost feel invisible tendrils between them, the stuff that had flowered so slowly, so quietly, that he'd never noticed until he'd tried to yank himself away. But now he was a sailor pulled under by a merman, lost in his hair, his body, drowning. *Oh yeah, very healthy, Jared!*

Toby cupped Jared's cheeks in his hands, his eyes earnest. "I finally figured out what I want, and you can't push me away. You won't, because I'll give you what *you* want."

"Toby, don't, please." Jared swallowed, feeling raw. He wanted to rub himself against Toby again, wanted to hide his face against Toby's warm neck.

Determination gritty in his tone, Toby continued. "I need to belong to you. You know it's right, and you know we've both felt that way right from the beginning, only I didn't understand it then."

"W-what!" Jared fell back, his larger muscled body trembling now as Toby pressed his fine-boned one closer, and despite the difference in their heights, he seemed to loom over Jared.

"I'm going to be your lover, Jared."

"*TIME, gentlemen; we're ready for you now.*"

Dazed, Jared let his robe fall, wearing nothing for this scene but his cock sock. He watched Toby's robe also falling. It seemed almost a primal act to watch him undress. Somehow his gaze got caught on the nipples he wanted to suckle like cherries, the smooth chest with light freckles, the unshaven lusty hair around Toby's sex.

"It's all yours, Jared," Toby whispered, reading him.

"You're not gay, Tobes!" Jared growled in a matching low tone, conscious they were not alone. "How can that work, a straight man surrendering to a gay man?"

Again a kind of tender amusement moved through Toby's eyes, as if he could see how hard he'd pushed Jared and was sorry. "You're already thinking about how to make it work."

Very firmly, Jared said, "*No.*"

Toby reached up and nipped his ear, ignoring the glances they were attracting. Probably he figured people would assume this was some form of rehearsal, which made Jared want to tear out his hair. The little imp made him want to spank him.

Oh shit!

THERE was a whisper of skin against skin, an almost-kiss as Jared cupped Toby's head and brushed his lips against him, playing the role of Aspen with his lover, Kelly. The lights glared down at the bed, and his confined penis rubbed against Toby's body in a way all too familiar. How often had he thought he couldn't bear it? Trying to stay Aspen when he wanted to rut for real.

But Toby still seemed calm, focused, bent on getting his way; his gaze intent on Jared in the moments when they waited for measurements to be taken or they had to adjust the angle or placement of their near naked bodies on the polyester satin bedding which translated into looking real on film.

"*Cut!* Okay, fellas, want a coke or something?" their director Simon asked, pulling ear plugs out and scrubbing a hand over his bearded chin. Someone coughed, free to do that now the moment was captured.

Jared almost fell off the bed in his haste to escape, reaching for his robe when he felt fingers against his tense shoulders, digging in. Then Toby leaned close to him, his body still bare, brushing gently against Jared's. "We need to talk," he whispered in Jared's ear.

Toby's lips brushed his skin. "I don't think that's a good idea," Jared choked, knowing he was blowing his image as the confident older man who could handle anything, but he wanted to crush Toby onto the bed for real. He wanted those slender, muscled legs wrapped around him. He wanted to fuck him, to have him.

"Jared, I need you." Toby's voice was sober, and against his better judgment, Jared responded, also needing to take care of Toby.

"All right, we'll talk, but Tobes, I don't think this is a sane idea."

Toby sat back on the bed, legs open, loosely encompassing Jared's body. The subtext didn't escape Jared, or the feeling of it being completely natural, not a pose Toby was assuming. "We'll talk here; there's something to be said for the ambiance."

"Oh, no, we won't," Jared said. "They're done with us until this afternoon. Go to your trailer, have a shower—preferably cold—and then we'll meet over lunch."

"Is that an order?" Toby whispered, his voice teasing, as if he deliberately wanted to mistake Jared. "A cold shower?"

Jared swallowed but couldn't stop himself, "Yes, it is. Oh, shit… what am I doing?"

Toby squeezed his hand, almost comforting. "It'll be all right, I promise."

Jared only laughed and put his head in his hands.

"VEGGIE?" Toby handed Jared a sandwich in the cafeteria as they stretched out their break from filming. Jared's hair was still damp, and Toby sat across the table from him as if respecting that his friend and co-star needed some room.

Jared took the offered plastic-wrapped food, uncovering it, not at all surprised Toby had snagged his preference. He ignored Toby's smirk when he no doubt took in the color in Jared's cheeks. He hardly ever blushed, but he'd been reliving their last exchange, picturing Toby showering under icy water because he commanded it.

"See?" As if reading his mind, Toby touched the back of his hand. His fingers were still chilly, as if he *had* taken that cold shower.

"You're seeing someone," Jared said, deciding to run through all the reasons why this couldn't work. "Aren't you?"

Toby shook his head but didn't enlighten Jared. "From my reading—"

"Wait! You were reading about stuff?" Jared chewed his lip. "About being with me?"

"Yeah." Toby blushed, but he still held Jared's gaze. "Sometimes I'd be online, and I'd think about you, and…." He shrugged. "Jared, this is all about you, how you make me—" He cleared his throat. "Your, um, affect on me."

Did that mean…? Toby had real feelings for him, like man-on-man feelings? Jared let out a breath, trying to shove that aside. It was too much like his fantasies.

"Okay, from my reading," Toby continued, "a submissive does not have to be the boyfriend of his Dom. They don't even have to have sex."

"No, they don't, but it's not that simple with us because I—I'm really looking for a boyfriend."

"Because you're in love with me." Toby's eyes were steady on Jared's face. And yet vulnerability lurked, as if Toby really needed to hear it.

Jared sighed, unable to deny Toby as always. "Yes."

With sudden enthusiasm, Toby said, "Jared, I thought I would stay over at your place a few nights a week."

Jared was shaking his head. "Whoa, wait a minute, what about Anita?" Jared couldn't imagine she had gone along with this. If Toby were his boyfriend, he sure as fuck wouldn't be okay with him being with someone else, never mind that Jared worked hard to be a spiritual person. There were limits.

"She moved into her own place." Toby swallowed. "Now she's working at that big law firm, my condo just wasn't big enough, I guess."

Jared stared, stunned. "I'm sorry. So you're—?"

"She wasn't happy about the 'vibe' between us," Toby confessed. "She said I should deal with my shit, that she deserved someone who was completely with her." Guilt moved over Toby's face. "I tried. Just lately I like spending time with you."

"Huh." But that wasn't quite the same thing as broken up, was it? "So is this about you suddenly being alone?"

Toby crumbled his own sandwich wrapper. "I'm not a complete loser, Jared. I like having my own place, but with both of you closing me out, I hurt."

Jared couldn't help but reach out, grasp Toby's hand. "Baby, you're not alone, but if this is some crazed rebound thing—"

"It's not." Toby leaned forward. "I've always felt safer and... *sexier* with you. I didn't want to face the last thing since...." He shoved back some of his blond sun-streaked hair. "I'm not gay, so what can it mean?"

"Toby, I have no idea," Jared confessed. "I hate seeing you hurt, but I don't know what to do. I've only ever been with other gay men."

"Please, let me give myself to you."

"Are you saying you want me to fuck you?" Jared demanded in a rough voice.

Soft, "Yes." And then, blue eyes fixed on Jared as if he was Toby's North Star, "Will I like it?"

Jared covered his eyes with a hand. "I can't do this."

"Jared!" Toby moved around the table and knelt beside his friend. When Toby leaned against him, his scent and his arms wrapped around Jared.

Jared put an arm around him. "Sit down, you jerk, and eat your sandwich."

Toby obeyed, this time sitting closer to Jared so his leg brushed against Jared's.

"I'm going away somewhere to talk to someone," Jared said, recognizing as he did that he was starting down a path he couldn't control. Soon he would be just as vulnerable as Toby.

Toby took his hand, squeezing silently, and for all his exasperation with how he was tearing up his life, Jared could see it wasn't calculated. Toby needed, and Jared wanted to be the answer to that need.

Chapter 4

JAI KIRAN put the phone down, anticipating seeing Jared again. Jared had been one of his best students, incredibly kind and gentle. He'd grappled a long time to integrate his desire for mild kink with his spiritual side but then found a unique way to paint them into his life with Jai's help.

He looked into the mirror, staring into his own solemn brown eyes, his face characterized by a kind of sleepy, wanton cast, as if he was always thinking about sex. Very useful in his chosen profession.

He hoped he could help Jared. The man had been in love with his best friend for a long time.

TOBY was sitting on Jared's bed, familiar Turkish Kelim wrapped around him. He couldn't seem to get warm; maybe it was the salty air breezing through Jared's open houseboat windows.

Or maybe it was that Jared was leaving him again.

He shoved back some of the tangled blond hair in his eyes. Okay, not really leaving him; Jared said he needed to talk to someone about what Toby had proposed, but all Toby could think about was what if this unknown person advised Jared to walk away from him?

Jared paused in packing the blue, purple, and green ribbon-woven knapsack he'd bought in Guatemala. It was typical of Jared, Toby reflected. His best friend surrounded himself with beautiful things:

blown glass, hand woven rugs, tactile stuff made by people, not by machines. Even when he got his floors polished or his couch reupholstered, he'd known the people doing the work and had talked to them extensively.

In contrast, Toby's home was almost sterile now Anita had removed all her pieces. He had a TV, a couch, a bed. But Toby had dozens of pictures hung in cheap brass frames on the wall of his living room, pictures of his friends, family, Anita, and a lot lately of Jared.

Jared had his head cocked; studying Toby like one of the idiosyncratic pieces he collected for his home, rubbing his bare chest, his fingers directly over his heart and the curve of the tail on his dragon tat which undulated between copper nipples.

Not for the first time, Toby was curious about it, but he had the sense the body art was connected to someone in Jared's past. That made him uneasy for some reason, acknowledging this part of Jared he couldn't touch. "It seems a shame sometimes when they cover that up with body make up," Toby said, a somber undertone to his voice he was unable to mask.

Jared shrugged. "I'm okay with it since it's not a part of Aspen's character." Then he gave Toby a direct look. "Toby, are you going to be all right?"

Even knowing it probably made him seem like a loser, Toby admitted, "I hate it when you go away."

Jared's brows rose as he sat down on the saffron hand-dyed bedding next to Toby. "You never told me that before." His voice was gentle, as if he knew Toby was embarrassed.

"It wasn't a big deal at first, but lately…." Toby leaned his body against Jared's and some of the tension in his gut relaxed. Jared put his arm around him.

"I'm glad you told me."

"It's not because I'll fall apart or anything," Toby grunted, wanting that clear. He'd miss Jared like fuck, not sleep well, okay, but he'd be working; he still put in time at the pool cleaning service since he didn't make a huge amount of money on the soap, not being one of the regulars like Jared. But right now it sounded pretty good, swishing a net through blue water, testing the pH, adding chemicals.

"I didn't think you would. You're very adaptable, do you know that? I think it's one of your strongest traits."

"That's good?" Now Toby's brows rose. It sounded more like how his stepfather said he had no drive, no ambition, just doing whatever was easiest.

"Jai, the man I'm going to see, would say you are like the bamboo—you bend, you grow in another aspect if you have to. It's a pretty formidable survival skill."

"Was he your boyfriend?"

Jared laughed. "You!"

Toby pulled his legs onto the bed and faced Jared. "Was he?"

"Jesus, Toby." Now Jared was blushing, shaking his head. "He was the man who taught me how to be comfortable with myself. Helped me achieve balance."

Toby reached out and traced the dragon, the curl of the tail, the wide dark watchful eye, the gathered flame riding on the tongue. "He gave you this."

"He was part of the experience. My dragon represents quiet courage and loyalty." Jared covered Toby's fingers, his warm brown eyes holding Toby's so suddenly Toby's heart was pounding.

Miserable, Toby prodded, "Is he going to tell you to drop me?"

"That's not how he works," Jared growled. "Toby, what is going on with us isn't wise, but I don't care. If you want me—I don't care."

Toby leaned forward, blindly groping, still awkward when he was kissing Jared as himself and not as his character. He couldn't hide behind a script. This was real. He was actually kissing another man. Shit!

His lips grazed Jared's, and he felt him take a deep breath, felt the rasp of Jared's beard shadow against his skin, something that took getting used to.

Jared whispered, "Drowning," and then he took command of their kiss, cupping Toby's jaw, loosening it, easing past Toby's lips with a warm tongue.

Toby's hands kneaded Jared's shoulders, looking for something, a place to hold onto, a place that felt comfortable. These weren't Anita's slender cool shoulders, but shoulders defined by muscle, the skin hot and silky to the touch. He moaned when Jared stroked his tongue with his, moved to shift closer, his legs embracing Jared's body like one of the purple flowers growing in Jared's herb patch, open.

Jared's hands slid lightly down his back and then cupped Toby's ass. It felt good, especially when Jared squeezed and then it felt amazing, zapping straight to his cock! Jared always made him feel good, and this was why Toby had wanted to get closer. Jared made him feel confident, sexy, and somehow he thought maybe he might be the key to Toby finally feeling good about himself as a man.

"Easy, baby, easy," Jared husked. But he didn't stop kissing Toby, as if he couldn't. He tasted, sipped, his tongue caressing, claiming and Toby let him. He was straight, wasn't he? But more and more he doubted. He'd only ever been curious, had a few fantasies, fine, but he'd lived his life as straight as the fucking lamppost on the wharf outside until now. Yet as Jared touched him, he was hard, hard for Jared.

He pressed his erection against Jared, moving closer, hands digging into his back now, heart galloping, skin prickling with sweat. This wasn't like with Anita when he had to do certain things and when he did, maybe she'd like them, or maybe she'd pick them apart. This was like being a wild creature, tasting, touching, flying.

"Sandalwood," he whispered, taking a moment to appreciate.

"Lots of men and women wear it," Jared answered, his big confident palm moved between their bodies, his pupils blown as he held Toby's gaze, as he stroked the fullness he found. "Jesus, Toby!"

Toby laughed, tears pricking his eyes because this was so fucking scary! How could he be feeling this way for Jared? It had started out with him just craving his warmth, just needing to secure it for himself, like a kitten searching for shelter out of the rain.

But he wasn't a fucking kitten. He was a man. And he wanted....

As if seeing he was a little unsteady, Jared leaned his forehead against Toby's. "We shouldn't be doing this now."

Toby laughed. "We shouldn't?"

"I mean...." Jared shook his head. "I should be figuring out how to keep us from getting hurt, from taking a wrong turn. If we keep heading down the highway at full speed, we might crash."

"I have a better idea; let's crash!" Toby's hands cupped Jared's neck. "I'm tired of not doing what I want. And in case you haven't noticed, I'm—" Heat stung his cheeks.

"Hard," Jared groaned. "Oh yeah." He looked pleased, proud, his dark hair falling over his face, giving him a boyish look. Adorable, Toby thought. *His.*

"As my boyfriend, can you leave me like this," Toby coaxed, watching heat flare in Jared's eyes. "Shouldn't you take care of me?"

"I haven't agreed to be your boyfriend yet, Toby!" Jared yanked Toby over on his stomach and his hand fell in a resounding smack. Then he paused, eyes wide, as if he hadn't planned it. "Oh shit."

Toby felt the red burn on his ass, looked over his shoulder to see it tilted up over Jared's lap. His erection twitched as he relived the sensation.

"Not bad," he said and then smiled when Jared flushed.

"I've wanted to do that for a while," Jared confessed with some feeling. "Ever since you started making me pull my hair out." But now he tugged Toby back up so they faced each other again. He cupped his cheek. "You're right; I don't want to leave you like this."

Toby pressed his face against Jared's neck. "I don't know what to do." His shoulders were tense, but there was only Jared, rubbing his back in gentle circles, reading him and waiting until he relaxed.

"You mean, you don't know what to do to *impress* me, right?" Jared clarified, pulling his head away so Toby was forced to meet his eyes.

"Yeah, I guess."

"Right now I just want you to like what I do. That's the kind of lover I am, Toby, more into bondage and driving my man crazy until he begs me to come." Jared smiled, his eyes lit, as if seeing into Toby's future.

The idea made Toby's eyes widen. "I think somehow I knew that."

Jared chewed his lip, considering. "Yeah, maybe somehow you did." Then he cocked a brow. "I could just watch while you took care of yourself."

Toby went even a brighter shade of red at the idea and his gaze dropped. He liked the thought, but he was embarrassed to admit it.

"Or, I could push you a little, go away with the memory fresh of a real act of submission," Jared rasped. "But only if you want. Do you hear me, baby?"

"Yes, I get it." He took a deep breath. "What do you want me to do?"

"I want you to strip and then kneel in front of me while I sit on the bed." Jared rubbed his shoulders. "Shit, and you need a safe word."

"Pistachio."

"What?" Jared looked taken aback.

"I have been doing my homework, Jared. I thought that one up since I don't like them much. Will I need it?" Toby stroked Jared's arm, finding it tense. "You take this so serious. Somehow it settles my first timer's nerves."

"I have no idea if you'll need it, but we aren't going to play unless I think you're totally safe, and that goes for how you feel inside, as much as your body." Jared stroked Toby's chest with a kind of gentle possessiveness.

"Okay, so if I can't handle something, I just say that word, right?"

"That's right, baby," Jared praised. He took a deep breath and sat back on the bed, his weight resting on his palms, his legs spread. "Toby, I'd like to see you."

Feeling like this was it, the big moment, Toby climbed to his feet. He pulled his tee shirt off quickly and then stood there, staring at Jared with wide eyes. Jared held his gaze calmly, but Toby could almost feel a force field surrounding them both made up of Jared's protection, Jared's warm desire. He was not indifferent to Toby and he wanted him to see it, as if knowing this was part of Toby's need.

"You've seen the rest, no big deal," he said, nevertheless trying to lighten the moment.

"It is a big deal to me," Jared admitted. "The first time was because no one told you to put on a cock sock for our nude scenes."

Toby groaned in memory. Would anyone on set ever forget that? Shit.

"But now it's real, it's you giving yourself to me, don't you think that's fucking huge?"

Toby's throat tightened. For all the control that Jared made no bones about liking to exercise, he was letting Toby see how much he wanted, how moved he was.

Toby unzipped his jeans and then shoved them off, standing there in the puddle of denim wearing only the black thong he'd bought because he thought it might please Jared.

"Whoa!" Now Jared sat up and when Toby put his fingers under it to remove it, he shook his head. "Do you mind leaving it on this time? It's sexy as hell."

Pleased that he had aroused his man, Toby gave a shy smile. "No, I'll wear it for you; I want to."

"It makes me want to spank you again, then squeeze your erection through the cloth," Jared said.

"Shit!" Toby breathed. And then as naturally as a leaf falling from a tree, he lowered his body, on his knees, sitting between Jared's spread thighs. He felt encompassed, safe, though he was nervous about Jared's intentions. What was he going to do to Toby?

But he wanted to mark the occasion, make it special for them both somehow. *I belong to him.*

He leaned forward and grazed his lips against Jared's knee. "Jared," he whispered.

Chapter 5

"WILL you wear a blindfold for me?" Jared leaned forward, hand resting casually on the knee Toby had kissed, holding Toby's eyes as if he already had him bound.

That look lit Toby up, so he licked his lips, heart pounding. A blindfold would mean he would be even more vulnerable, unable to see what Jared was going to do with him. "Yes, for you, Jared." *For you alone.*

"Thank you." Jared kissed him and a small yellow ball of happiness expanded in Toby's chest.

"Wait one moment. I need to gather a few things."

Toby gave a jerky nod, head falling forward. He took a deep breath, and then another, trying to relax.

"I won't tell you not to be nervous, but try to remember I want you to enjoy this experience." Jared squeezed his shoulder as he climbed to his feet.

"I'll try." Toby appreciated how Jared was both touching and talking to him. It meant that when he fell to his knees, it seemed inevitable. Not because of the stuff in his life he was still trying to sort out. Being submissive wasn't about that, he didn't think. This was something that had just been brewing between them, the cocktail of their personalities slowly building, gathering pressure... and here they were.

He wasn't sure if he was supposed to watch what Jared was gathering, but Jared hadn't forbidden it, so he tracked him out of the corner of his eyes. The open blue shirt was a good color against Jared's smooth tanned skin, the fuchsia surfer's shorts covered with creamy hibiscus flowers. Jared liked to wear the same bright colors he decorated with.

"Good boy." Jared opened several drawers in his bamboo dresser, first lighting some incense, coiling sandalwood and roses into the damp sea air that always seemed to breathe on the floating house. The softer scents relaxed the ambiance and Toby found himself focusing on Jared's face as he adorned a bowl of potpourri with fresh lemon oil, stirring the mix with one finger. Everything he did was about ceremony, about creating welcome, making Toby feel like an important guest invited for a banquet.

Next, he moved on to kneel by his altar, bending closer to pick up some scattered polished stones. Toby found himself craning his neck to get a look, curious. What struck him was that his new lover hadn't made an immediate trip to his toy drawer.

Jared reached out and touched his statue of Kwan Yin. "I ask for compassion," he whispered. "For myself and for Toby."

"You begin *this* with a prayer?" Toby asked, eyes widening. He thought he knew everything about Jared, but this secret side was only shown to a boyfriend.

"You're very important to me, Toby," Jared said. "If I'd had more time to prepare I might have fasted, meditated."

"For me?" But a smile curved his lips. *Jared, you romantic dork.*

"Of course for you." Jared paused and gave Toby a look he'd never offered, not even as his character Aspen. Smoldering, possessive, but with a hint of *do you really like me?* "I take care of myself, my home, and I always imagined if I had a boyfriend... well, I'd take care of him as well. Not because he'd need me to do that, but because we'd both enjoy it."

Toby cleared his throat. It was weird, kneeling here next to nude but feeling oddly homey. Maybe it was because Jared was fucking around with incense and Kwan Yin and not dildos and nipple clamps.

Jared reached into his low bamboo bedside table and pulled out a silk scarf dyed in oblongs of vivid oranges and turquoises. Everything he owned seemed to be a delight to the senses, so Toby's lips parted when Jared touched cool chiffon to his shoulder. He shivered in response and Jared smiled, a sexual smile that said, *I touch you, and you react, and we both enjoy it.*

"I feel like a Chinese fire cracker you're setting off."

Jared leaned his forehead against Toby's and his nuzzle was soon reciprocated. *It's not so different from being with Anita—affection, cuddling even!* Toby thought in surprise.

"I like setting off the ones with a looong fuse," Jared said, arching a brow. "I'll try to give you that." He placed the scarf on the bed and then his face sobered as he offered Toby some stones, milky blue and gray-brown chunks, polished to the touch.

"What?" Toby wrinkled his brow.

"Look, Toby, some of what I share with you might seem like new age bullshit." Jared's face heated in a blush. He rubbed his eyebrow ruefully.

"I'm here. I'm listening." Jared had been patient with his feelings. Toby didn't want to hurt him.

"This is Larimar, from the Caribbean. It's reputed to help people dealing with stress and anxiety." Jared held Toby's eyes. "I just want you to have it while I'm away, maybe put it on the bedside table so it's close to you while you sleep. Even if you think it's bogus, I'd appreciate it."

"Here?" Toby felt that cold dread poking him, remembering that Jared was leaving him. "You want me to crash at your place?"

"I thought maybe you'd stay after I left, yes. This place—it's part of me. It would make me feel better if I knew you were here." Grave eyes examined Toby's face.

"You don't want Anita seeing me while you're gone," Toby guessed.

Jared put the nuggets in Toby's hand, clasping it and then caressing the back with his thumb. Toby caught his breath at the tiny explosion of sensation. Fuck! Jared wasn't holding back, treating him as he would a lover—and Toby liked it.

"Toby." Jared reached up and brushed the lump on his shoulder with gentle, meaningful fingers. "I want to know what happened here. I mean, you aren't with me because you need to be rescued, not after the way you—" He coughed. "—pursued me."

Toby's gaze dropped and his face heated. Damn. He'd thought the color had faded. "I don't want to talk about it," he mumbled. "Oh fuck, all right. We had a fight, and she threw her hair brush at me because I said I was going to go see you. Satisfied? It wasn't nice, but it was kind of about us breaking up." Toby swallowed. "I wish it hadn't been so upsetting."

Jared studied him. "All right. But please stay or I'll probably call you too often."

"Do it anyway. And just imagine me sleeping in your bed if your friend Jai advises you to dump me." Toby's lips quirked.

"Meow!" Jared covered his eyes. "You have a very predatory kind of ruthlessness."

"I want you to come back for me." There he'd done it. Now he was as naked as his body, but Jared only took him in his arms, so Toby experienced the shelter of his warm clothed body, the smell of sandalwood, his controlled touch.

"Don't go," Toby whispered.

JARED placed his lips against the little lump on Toby's shoulder. "I'll come back. You know I'll come back."

"Of course you will." Toby shrugged. "I know that!"

"I mean, I'll come back for you." Seeing he would get nowhere trying to convince Toby, who was strung tight, who needed time—they *both* just needed time—Jared lifted the temporarily abandoned scarf. "You'll like this," he promised.

Toby remained still, his face slightly raised, as if holding onto his sight as long as possible. Jared sat back on his heels, taking a moment to consider him. Fuck, he'd never imagined Toby would be here with him, fitting into the one part of his life he'd managed to keep in shadow, hidden from his best friend.

"Take some deep breaths," Jared advised, squeezing Toby's hand. It was a big deal, giving up your eyes.

"I'm all right," Toby said.

Jared leaned forward, capturing Toby's lips, feeling his new lover's muscles tense in surprise. *Yes, this is what it will be like, baby. Relax and let yourself flow with it.*

"I'm going to gather a few other things," he said and saw a ripple go through Toby's body. Anticipation? Curiosity? Jared smiled since he intended this to be fun. "I will briefly be in the galley kitchen, but I'll leave the door open and let you know when I return."

Toby nodded.

"Are you comfortable? You don't need to hold that kneel," Jared said and he reached out and gently helped Toby arrange himself on his ass. He couldn't resist spreading Toby's thighs and cupping his erection through the black silky fabric of the thong, running a fingernail over Toby's length. "Mmmmm, very nice. Is this for me?" he whispered, letting the purr of approval color his voice. He could imagine what Toby was experiencing right now, living for every word, senses blooming at every touch. From the wanton way he thrust against Jared's hand, it wouldn't take much to get him off, either.

"Yes, it's for you," Toby's voice was breathless. "Jared."

Jared took a deep breath, wishing he could enjoy Toby's body. It would be delicious to fuck him while having him lean against the side of the bed, Toby's round ass high. Or maybe he'd make him grab his ankles….

Whoa. That couldn't happen now. He didn't want to scare or offer Toby any discomfort and he'd never been with a man who was a virgin to being with other men. All his lovers had been experienced and had known Jared's reputation. He usually preferred confident men, men who wouldn't expect emotional attachments and just wanted a bit of light play. He knew he was a bit of a control freak, so he couldn't help but be amused at how Toby was totally fucking with that, pursuing *him*.

"Be right back." He touched Toby's cheek lightly.

"ARE you ready to try this with me?"

Toby laughed. "I don't know! This is big."

"Yeah." Jared sympathized. This was a fantasy too poignant, too close to him. His best dream and his worst nightmare, packed into the lean dynamite of Toby Rafferty. "Did you and Anita ever...?" He swallowed, not wanting to know *anything* about his rival for Toby's affections, but he usually liked to have some idea of a lover's past history.

"Use incense and Kwan Yin? No. Not her thing." Toby's voice was both amused and sad.

He's not over her. But I can give him time. Maybe.

"Play with me, Toby," Jared enticed, taking a dripping ice cube off the plate he'd gathered in the kitchen. "Just play."

Toby's body arched in shock as Jared grazed the cube against one pointing nipple. "Oh shit! Ice?"

"You can find all you need for a little play in a well-stocked kitchen," Jared teased. "Well, my kitchen anyway."

"Not what I expected." Toby was panting as Jared skimmed the ice over his other nipple. Jared noted that his erection hadn't subsided, but a wet spot had bloomed where Toby's penis prodded the cloth. He licked his lips, wishing he could taste Toby, wanting to take that fullness into his mouth, maybe with his new lover tied and helpless so he could make a feast of him.

He touched the cube to Toby's lips, and when Toby licked them in response, he leaned close to steal a kiss. Toby's hands had been gripping his thighs, as if bracing himself, but now they reached up and wrapped around Jared's arms, asking him to stay close, to sustain the kiss.

Jared was more than happy to please his beautiful boy, licking cool water, delving inside, penetrating and claiming with measured control so that Toby's fingers dug into his skin, impatient.

While he tasted Toby, he took the cube, dissolving fast in the heat between them, and skimmed the top of Toby's cock with it through the saturated cloth of his thong.

Toby's head fell back. "Oh Jared." He shivered, trembling as Jared tormented him skillfully.

"I want to try something. Will you trust me?" Jared was panting now, moved by Toby's submission.

"Yes, go ahead."

"I need you on your hands and knees." Jared helped Toby into position, firm, caressing Toby's arms and legs affectionately.

He pulled Toby's thong down, stroking the raised moons of his ass. "Fucking gorgeous!" he praised. "Toby, shit, you have no idea."

"What are you going to do?" Toby widened his legs and Jared wondered if he wanted to be deliberately a tease, showing a glimpse of the back of his heavy, hanging balls and the length of his cock, sliding free of the thong now to flex in reaction to Jared's every touch.

"This." Carefully Jared opened Toby's body and then circled the virgin dimple he found there with the ice.

Toby shuddered, shouting now. *"Fuck!"*

"Will you take it?" Jared was suddenly breathless. Already the games between them were spinning out of control.

"Yes," Toby choked and then shivered wildly as Jared inserted the melted sliver of ice, broaching him.

Chapter 6

"JARED!" Toby huffed out a breath since the ice was becoming uncomfortable. He contracted around it, and Jared pulled it free. He heard him shift and then—

Warm, wet liquid.

"Green tea," Jared whispered. Once again he put his warmed lips to Toby's chilled body. Toby huffed, at first experiencing heat, silken lips, but now it translated into making him want to come. Chilly, warm, silky, *intense.*

Jared's big hand cupped the back of his neck, smooth, controlling. "Put your head on the floor, Toby, and brace yourself."

Toby obeyed, flushing under the screen of his blindfold since the position made his ass stick up even more prominently; he pictured how he must look, Jared's total slut, but it only seemed to turn him on, as did the thought, *I'm his to play with.*

He'd never imagined he could find this so arousing, giving himself this way. He'd gone along with friends and family, the currents in his life, because of his own basic breezy good nature. If he had to put his foot down, he did, as he had about taking the job on the soap and then maintaining a close friendship with his gay co-star.

When he'd had this impulsive idea, he'd just been flying by instinct. He hadn't been sure how he'd really feel, but the horoscope he'd read the day his girlfriend had left him said that he had to risk himself, his ego, and move to scary new ground for what would truly fulfill him.

Aching, alone, for some reason as he'd read that, a single name popped into his head: *Jared.* What he hadn't known then and still didn't know was how to make it work. But maybe Jared knew.

JARED alternated the ice and green tea at gentle intervals, just grazing Toby with the sliver, so it wasn't too much. Ultimately what came across was that Jared was in command of what Toby was experiencing. If he wanted to mouth him with lips warmed by tea, he would.

Yet it was Toby's choice to let him do that.

The blindfold also was his choice, and it enhanced the sensations so they seemed to bloom larger in his body.

"Are you comfortable?"

"Yes," Toby said.

"Good. You look so sexy, baby." Jared's hand caressed his back, easing pockets of tension so that Toby's arousal was somehow magnified. "I ache to put my cock here." Fingers brushed his dimple. "To use you."

Toby's heart pounded. He swallowed. He shouldn't like that Jared wanted to use him, should he? He wasn't used to thinking of himself in that context, as if he were sexy... slutty. "I'm yours, Jared."

Jared's hand came down, cracking his left ass cheek and Toby jumped, moaning since his body tightened on the tiny kernel Jared had used to torment him with. That was punishment? He was getting a real yen for Jared to spank him, and he was sure the taste he was being given was deliberate.

"Not yet, Toby, but while I'm away I'll get you started on preparing yourself for me if you want a cock inside you," Jared said firmly.

Toby wondered what that would involve, but he didn't ask since he sensed Jared wouldn't answer him. Part of what he was doing seemed to be about the surprise, about taking Toby off-guard and into an erotic new world.

"One moment," Jared said, his deep voice husky so that Toby knew he wanted him, wanted him badly. It made that yellow ball in his chest expand. He felt sexy right now, all Jared's attention focused on him. And he didn't feel like he was missing something like he had previously in his relationship with Anita. With her, he knew it had been his fault, which is why he'd felt so lousy during their fight. Part of him had never been there with her.

He heard Jared opening something and then gasped, head arching up, as cool liquid spattered over his back and down the crack of his ass. His penis continued to throb, heavy with the need to come, even as he shivered violently at the sudden shock.

"Milk and...." Jared paused and Toby moaned as he laved something thick and room temperature against his dimple. "Honey."

The idea that Jared had adorned him this way made Toby shift his legs wider. "Jared?"

"The better to feast on you," Jared whispered and then his lips were on Toby's back, his hands opening him, making Toby wildly aware that until Jared, no one had ever looked at this part of him.

As if sensing Toby's tension, Jared rubbed his face against Toby's skin. "You're beautiful."

Disbelieving, "Even there?"

"Especially there! I want to taste."

Toby licked dry lips. He wasn't sure he wanted this. It just seemed so... gay. Something that he'd never done with Anita. Yet so far everything with Jared had felt good. Toby decided to try to shove aside this new insecurity that he was experiencing with Jared now they were becoming lovers. "Okay."

He felt Jared smile against his skin. And then Jared spread him open and his breath touched the place where he'd only lightly toyed with the sliver of ice and warm tea. Toby was still chilled there, so when a warm tongue licked him, he gave a muffled growl.

"Oh, baby, we're going to have so much fun with this part of you," Jared promised. "You'll want me to put something inside you all the time." Jared stroked his back, his arm reaching down to cup Toby's submissively lowered head as he continued licking Toby's opening. Toby shuddered, sudden surprising tears pricking his eyes under the blindfold when Jared's tongue penetrated him. It was—oh. He couldn't—!

"Jared!" He panted and sweat broke out on his forehead.

Jared immediately stopped. "What is it, Toby?"

"I thought I could take that, but I can't," Toby said flatly.

He felt Jared pull away, imagining he must feel rejected, but it wasn't that! Toby made a hopeless sound. "I mean, I just can't right now. I thought I could but—" It felt *too* good, unlike anything he'd ever experienced. And it had freaked him out.

Jared pulled him to his knees and folded him in his arms. Toby clung, panting. After a moment, Jared removed the blindfold, and Toby was looking into familiar concerned brown eyes, not the husky-voiced master he'd obeyed when he'd given up his sight.

"I... something else is wrong too." He was embarrassed, even knowing this was what he was supposed to feel from what he'd read. "I have to come. I absolutely have to come!" His head dipped, shamed. He'd failed. Jared wouldn't reward him. Already he'd failed.

"That's good you told me," Jared said, giving a breathless laugh himself, but Toby could clearly hear the relief. "I don't want to scare you away. Oh God, you can't imagine how much I don't want to do that!" Then Jared reached down and clasped Toby's cock through the silk thong, just holding it firmly between their bodies. "Give yourself to me, Toby. This is mine now, and I need to know when my slut needs to come."

The word *slut* made Toby's breath stall in his chest. He'd felt as if Jared was gently leading him into seeing himself that way. Was it okay to like hearing it? Was it really okay to see himself this new way? "Your... slut needs to come now," he pleaded. "Please let me, Jared. I know I didn't do it right."

"Shhhhh, you're everything I want, can't you see that?" Jared swallowed, his amber eyes full of feeling. "Then do it," he prodded. "I want you to perform for me. I want your come on my hand."

"Jared." Toby choked on the word. He felt a flush roar up through his body, tightening his balls, splaying his fingers, tearing a cry from his throat, and then he was spilling, spilling, spilling. He was Jared's slut now, and he loved his hand on his cock, telling him what to do, taking control. "Jared! Thank you, God, so good!" He collapsed, and Jared collapsed with him, and he lay there, in a pool of his own come,

with his new lover's body warmly cupping him from behind, the prod
of Jared's erection against his bare ass.

TOBY felt Jared pull away, and he bit his lip to keep himself from
asking where he was going. As the glow faded, quicker than Toby
liked, Toby's doubts came back. He tried to stay in the moment, in
being—for the first time in his life—someone's slut, but Jared leaving
made him feel like he'd raced over a bridge, only to find half of it
missing.

The longer he thought about it, the more it seemed as if he'd
failed somehow. Jared was still leaving, despite what they'd
exchanged. Toby had fucked up, had ruined his one chance to belong to
Jared because of the feelings that had walloped him when Jared put his
tongue inside Toby for the first time. Now he was going to go away,
meet up with this Jai character, the one who had somehow given Jared
his oh-so-cool dragon tat, and Jai would advise Jared to dump Toby.

He jumped when a hand touched his shoulder, squeezing gently.
"Will you sit up?"

"Jared, man, I don't know why I—"

"*Quiet,*" Jared commanded. That tone, his eyes, and body posture
stilled him, and instinctively Toby obeyed.

Jared dipped a sea sponge into a basin of water. As Toby blinked
in disbelief, Jared traced the warm water over his chest, rubbing away
the sweat, the remnants of milk and honey, and come on Toby's body.
Dazed, Toby didn't refuse when Jared spread his legs so he had better
access to his softened penis, cleaning it so thoroughly that Toby's body
stiffened with renewed interest. His lips parted as Jared explored him.

"I'd like to bend down and suck that," Jared said. "Wouldn't you
like that? I want to take you completely."

"Jared."

"But I digress." A mischievous spark lived in his brown eyes. "I
want to clean your back and ass. Are you okay with that?"

Toby opened his lips, again wanting to apologize, but Jared took
his chin in his fingers. "Don't talk right now, Tobes. This is for you.

Just concentrate on your breathing and how I make you feel. Can you do that?"

Toby took a deep breath and nodded and when Jared guided him back on his hands and knees, although he blushed when his semi-erect cock wobbled with obvious need between them, especially when Jared touched that forbidden place.

He felt the first words—probably the wrong words—that he might have uttered crumble like pebbles, falling aside. *Don't talk right now, Tobes.*

"I love you," Jared said simply, and Toby's eyes stung again.

"I don't know how to love anyone." The confession was something Toby had never admitted aloud, but the ache had lived under his breastbone for a long time.

"Yes, you do." Jared finished with the sea sponge and patted Toby dry with a soft Egyptian cotton towel. "Who better than your best friend to know that."

JARED lit a candle by the bed, placing the stones he'd shown Toby earlier there. Arms wrapped around his legs, Toby watched.

"There's plenty of food in the fridge now, or you can order in. If you do, you have to go up to the gate and get it there," Jared said. He rubbed his tanned hands against his jeans, as if he was also riding some powerful feelings.

"How long will you be gone?" Toby asked.

"Have to be back for work on Tuesday." It was Thursday night. Shit!

"That long?"

"Jai isn't someone you visit in a rush."

Oh. Toby wanted to ask Jared if he and Jai would have sex since they were still so cozy, but he was afraid of Jared's answer. He hated Jai already.

"Walk with me to my car?" Jared offered his hand, and Toby reached for it, unable to refuse though resentment and loss still ached in his chest. He knew he had no right to feel it, but somehow it wouldn't go away.

Jared closed but didn't lock his door, pausing for a moment to look at the setting sun over the water, low in the horizon.

"I guess you'll miss your house."

"I'll miss *you.*" Jared pulled him into his arms, drawing Toby's back to his muscled chest, and held him.

"Jared!" Toby huffed.

"What?" Jared blinked. "Oh, the cuddling." His arms fell away. "You're afraid someone will see us, right?"

Toby was probably totally driving him away, but maybe it was for the best. He wanted what he did with Jared to be a secret. He sighed, wondering how the hell this was going to work.

They walked up the wharf side by side, Jared's bag slung over his shoulder like a sailor bound on a long voyage. When they reached Jared's baby blue DeSoto, he shoved the bag in the back and took a moment to rest his forehead against Toby's. "All right?" he asked softly.

The words escaped before he could stop himself. "I'll make it right! I'll do it better next time."

"Toby," Jared said, his eyes somber, like the sun swallowed by the ocean. "There is no right way. Maybe there is an 'our' way, but for right now I'm not sure." He cupped Toby's face. "I wish I could kiss you goodbye."

Toby swallowed, wanting that too, but before he could ask, Jared had turned away, climbing into the driver's seat. Toby wrapped his arms around himself, feeling the chill of approaching night.

Jared looked up at Toby as he started his car and swung it free of its habitual parking space. The last Toby saw of him were his eyes holding Toby's in the reflection of Jared's rearview mirror.

Chapter 7

TOBY rubbed his eyes, his heart pounding as he strode to answer the knock at Jared's door. Could it be Jared back already? Maybe the key he gave Toby was the only one he had so—

Anita.

Toby stared at his ex-girlfriend through the heron-etched glass of Jared's door. The moment of his latest failure with Jared washed over him like acid. He'd had Jared's tongue *inside* him but he couldn't.... And then Jared had left him, as Anita had left him.

He knew it was bogus, but somehow both events were tied up in his head right now. He guessed this was why Jared hadn't wanted him to see her while he was away; maybe he'd known that Toby would be feeling off balance after throwing himself at Jared, after pursuing something so wild, so forbidden.

"Toby, for God's sake! Aren't you going to let me in?" Anita chided, peering at him through the glass and for the first time, Toby cursed the fact that Jared had such an airy home, that it had so many windows. If he were behind a plank of wood, he could pretend not to be here.

"Hey, Anita," Toby said, striving for a light tone as he unlocked the brass lock.

"I knew you'd be here," she said, shoving past him. She smelled of honeysuckle and ivory soap, her hair in a ponytail pulled back from her tanned face. She looked like the wholesome girl next door.

"Jared's not here," he said, immediately on the defensive despite how neutral she'd always seemed about his friendship with Jared, except when she was annoyed that Toby spent so much time with him.

Anita was looking around the room speculatively. "Quite the little nest he's built for someone."

"For himself, Anita. He likes to decorate to please himself."

"It's a cliché for someone of his orientation, isn't it?" Again, Toby heard that careful neutrality.

Toby blew out some air and reminded himself that if Jared were here, he'd just laugh. Anita's pokes never seemed to bother him. He only seemed to get angry if she was tough on Toby, but he knew he wasn't the perfect boyfriend.

"I wonder what his bedroom's like?" Before Toby could stop her, she was heading down Jared's hallway, past the bathroom into the light-filled bedroom. "Have you been in here?"

"Hey, shit! This is private, Nita." Toby hurried after her, grasping her arm in the center of the room.

She shook him off. "An altar? So he's one of those new age types?"

"Jesus, Anita, way to be tolerant," Toby said in disgust.

"Oh, come on. And he's not my friend." She crossed her arms, skin he'd stroked with fine blond hairs. He couldn't help that immediately an image popped into his head of Jared stroking *his* arms as he—

Shit! He was blushing.

"So you finally went for it," Anita said flatly. "Jesus, Toby, I hope you don't let your stepfather know."

"I don't know what you mean." Toby stared at Kwan Yin, craving some of Jared's serenity. The ghost of the incense he'd lit before he'd left still lingered: rose, sandalwood.

"Don't bullshit me, Toby. The only reason he didn't get his hands on you before was because you were living with me. Now you're on the rebound. I bet he couldn't wait." She shook her head. "And I was sure you'd pursue me as soon as we broke up."

Toby laughed nervously, breaking out in a sweat. He almost never won any fights with Anita, just felt uneasy and sick and eventually asked for her forgiveness, even if he wasn't sure what he'd done wrong. "You're wrong. I pursued *him*."

Anita shook her head. "I tried to convince your parents it was just a job, being on that soap, but you've been spending more and more time with him. It's not just a buddy thing. I didn't want to see it, but why did you think I finally broke up with you?"

"He makes me feel good." Shit, his face was on fire. He wanted her to go! He'd hated the fight they'd had, and now he was uneasy as she opened up and showed him some of her thinking. She'd thought he had a thing for Jared? How was it she'd sensed that and he'd been so clueless? And he missed Jared so fucking much, needed to know they were still friends at least after the botched first attempt, but he hadn't heard from him all day. Probably his friend Jai was keeping him busy. Fuck.

Anita brushed closer, circling him, studying his face. Toby felt as if his whole encounter with Jared was written there. "You know what I think happened? I think you couldn't do it, couldn't give him what he wanted."

Toby crossed his arms. "I don't want to talk to you about this."

"It's okay. This is what I wanted you to face, don't you understand?" She reached down and touched him. The grip was familiar, something he was used to responding to. Love feelings, sex feelings, no confusion here. He'd been with her so long.

He shook his head. No. They'd broken up. He was pursuing Jared now. He couldn't—

His cock hardened at her touch, just like always. But he didn't want—why did this still happen with her?

"Don't." He took her hand, clasping it. "You broke up with me."

She stared up into his eyes. "Break-up sex is the best sex. Don't you know that?"

"What? You're jealous."

"For years, I've seen the way he looked at you, and you loved it. Don't bullshit me that you didn't."

"So what if I did?" He felt like she was peeling away all his layers, touching him places he was raw and questioning. *Scared.*

Anita had used his moment of distraction to move closer. She stroked him again and he squeezed his eyes shut, humiliated. But he still cared about her deeply, he hadn't had time--

"No! We finished it, Nita. And I can't. Not here."

Anita was kissing him, and he hated himself because he was responding. Her hair, her skin—all of it was familiar, anchoring. Unlike with Jared, he wasn't uncertain and afraid. He knew what to do, knew what she liked.

"Toby." She was on him, rubbing herself against him now and his fingers were under her shorts, finding her wet, even as his heart twisted, sick.

Mendocino, California

JARED eased himself into the wooden hot tub, rented by the half hour on the waterfront in Mendocino. He looked up at Jai Kiran, his half Indian friend and sometime lover.

Jai also had a dragon tattoo, his snaking across one bicep. It was golden, talons stretching over smooth skin. He was shorter than Jared, only around five seven, with long dark hair cut in uneven shafts, giving him an urchin-on-the-street look despite the smooth muscles of his slight body. His demurely lowered lids were lined with kohl, something Jared personally found incredibly sexy.

Everything about him was enticement, which was fitting in one of the top male escorts in the state. And yet he was also formidable in martial arts, and taught Sanskrit at a local college.

"I missed you so much!" Jai said now, giving a sigh of relief as he sank into the water. The place was privately screened, and many times Jared and Jai had gone into the water nude, but this time Jared had left on a pair of Maui trunks. Jai had picked up on the signal, leaving on a black silk loin cloth that molded his erection, barely covering lusty black hair around his cock. "Especially lately, since I've been worried about you."

"Me too." Jared's head fell back, his hair floating around him as he looked up at the sky. He'd driven all night and into the day to get here, all the time fighting the need to turn back, to go to Toby. "I always feel more myself when I'm with you, Jai."

"Me too." Jai smiled as he repeated Jared's words. "Is it all right to move a little closer?"

For an answer, Jared put an arm around the smaller man, this special person who had grown up alone on the streets of Chinatown in San Francisco, who had taught him about an odd blend of spirituality, meditation, and sex. Incredible sex! He shook his head, rueful. But he couldn't enjoy this trip the way he usually did, indulging in sweaty, soothing relief with Jai. He had someone now at last, his special someone. Maybe.

"So how is Toby doing?" Jai asked, raising an eyebrow as he shook his hair, the heavy locks clinging to his strong neck.

Jared took a moment to appreciate him, thinking Jai looked a bit like a Kouros statue of a boy from ancient Greece. But despite the youthful sensuality of his appearance, he was wiser than he seemed, able to listen to his friends, to care for them.

Jared shoved his own hair off his forehead, wondering when he'd ever put one over on his delicate teacher; of course, Jai had to have guessed that what had brought Jared here all of a sudden was Jared's secret crush. "He came to me with the most incredible proposal."

"Um?" Jai settled back against Jared's long arm, as if content to enjoy the moment, their closeness, without expectation, like a cat simply enjoying a sunny spot.

"He wants to be my lover."

Jai's eyes popped open and Jared laughed. "Yeah? Does he know about your enjoyment of tying men up sometimes?" Faint color touched his dusky skin since Jared had often tied him up, and they'd both certainly enjoyed it.

Jared sighed.

"You're afraid of letting him down, since that is your path to pleasure." Jai took Jared's hand, squeezed it.

"I think...." Jared's throat tightened and he closed his eyes. "I already did."

TOBY was huddled under the Kelim in Jared's dark living room. The lights were off and only the setting sun provided any illumination.

Anita had left hours ago.

He rubbed his eyes, the same thoughts chasing through his head. He remembered when he'd wanted to get a puppy a year into dating her. He'd still been living at home, but he'd ached to have something to love, to call his own. He'd brought home a beautiful, affectionate golden retriever. He'd loved taking that puppy out with him, having it in his room at night, something dependant on him even if he was a screw-up sometimes, not getting great grades, not being a perfect boyfriend. But he'd had less and less time with all the demands on him, so he'd come from his part time job sometimes to find the dog had messed in his bedroom.

He'd wanted to keep him so much, but Anita had talked him out of it. She'd been calm, sensitive that Toby really loved the dog, but she'd nudged him that he was being selfish, that the puppy needed to be walked more, needed more than he could give.

A month after he'd gotten it, brought it home proudly, it had gone to one of her friends.

She'd been right in that case, as much as it had hurt him at the time. Right to intervene. The dog had had a much better life. Was this what she was doing now? She hadn't said anything before she'd left, after they'd....

Shit, he'd violated Jared's home, his trust!

In the same room where they had just begun to explore the stuff between them, Toby had fucked Anita. Fucked her on the floor beside Jared's bed, given her pleasure, though for some reason he couldn't stay hard enough to come inside her. But that didn't mean anything. How could he have done such a thing?

He put his head on his knees. He'd have to tell Jared. What if Anita told him? Would she do that?

His mind went round and round, trying to find a solution that didn't hurt anyone, especially Jared. Jared had possessed serious reservations about being with Toby before, he'd even left him, was probably sleeping with that Jai guy who had to know a lot more about pleasing another man than Toby did.

He was sure to tell Jared that Toby's idea was crazy, that he could not be the lover Jared needed.

And he'd be right. Look at what Toby had done!

The ache wouldn't go away. *Please forgive me, Jared.*

Like a lost spirit haunting the floating house, Toby climbed to his feet and returned to the bedroom. The bed was still the way it had been when he'd been on it with Anita, before he'd instinctively moved her to the floor, away from where Jared slept. Toby gathered up the sheets, the silk spread, tearing them off the bed like the mistake he wished he could undo.

Panting now, he went to the closet which held Jared's double washer and dryer and piled them inside, making himself stop a minute to read the instructions for the silk spread—he didn't want to ruin Jared's things. When he was done, he returned to the bedroom and opened all the windows looking out at the horizon, letting in the burn of sea air.

Then he knelt by the altar for the first time, not knowing much about Kwan Yin except Jared had once told him she was the Chinese goddess of compassion.

He reached out and touched her face, wishing he could find a still place inside himself. Maybe he should have asked Jared to help him learn how to meditate instead of the other stuff. Would have been safer. Sometimes with Jared, he'd almost been happy, as if he was closer to being in the right place. But now that was over.

All that remained was to wait for Jared, to tell him it was over.

Chapter 8

JARED paced on the balcony lined with driftwood outside Jin's guest room. Various wind chimes made of beach glass, shells, and scrap metal clanged softly as if they were as restless as he was.

Between his legs, his sex ached, and what he really wanted right now was Toby waiting for him in his bed. He wanted to press his wrists face up, mesh his palms to Toby's, and looking into his wide blue eyes, penetrate him.

He moaned softly at the sharp picture that came to mind. This thing with Toby had only made his fantasies worse, more three dimensional so that he could hear the soft sounds Toby made when he was hard, picture his face again as he cried out *thank you, God, so good!*

Oh shit. Now his balls were tight as he ached with the need to find his mate, mount him and pound into him. He leaned forward, gripping the driftwood that wrapped around the balcony. He smelled the cool sea air, much chillier up here than in the waters near San Diego where he lived.

Needing to connect with Toby, Jared took his phone out of his pocket, hit speed dial and waited. And waited. The pause made him tense and his instincts whispered that he needed to talk to Toby. Now.

"Jared's place," Toby finally answered, his voice raspy, deadened.

Jared frowned. "Tobes, you okay, man?"

Toby cleared his throat. "Yeah, I... went for a swim is all. Just got back in the house."

"Are you chilled? Put the phone down and wrap yourself in a towel if you need to," Jared ordered, automatically needing to care for Toby despite the distance.

"Ja–red. I'm okay."

But he didn't sound okay. Shit! "I have some purple cone flowers that I dried from my patio in the kitchen. Make some herb tea and add them to it."

"Why would I do that?" Toby's voice was a little lighter, indulgent like a lover's. Jared liked that, liked the intimate sound of it in his ear, probably too much, considering everything they had to work out.

"It's a natural source of *Echinacea angustifolia* which can give your immune system a real boost. You sound as if you need it."

"I miss *you*. Will Echina-whatever help with that?"

"No, it's not good for easing, um, heartache." Jared was trying to do the right thing, spend some time with Jai, decompress, and talk about his options with Toby. In the end, this was the most correct path to take, so why did he feel like he was screwing everything up? "Do you have those stones by the bed?"

"Not going in there," Toby mumbled.

"Oh, I thought you were going to sleep in my bed."

"I just don't want to, okay?"

Whoa. "Sure, the couch is comfortable. Are you in the great room now?"

"Yeah. I'm trying to decide if I have enough energy to watch a DVD. How's Jai?" Jared would have been deaf not to hear the shades of jealousy in Toby's tone. It was inappropriate from his boyfriend, who needed to learn who Jared was, learn to have faith in him, but that couldn't happen overnight. As friends, co-workers, they'd learned to trust each other. But as lovers....

Jared sighed, then said evenly, "Jai's doing fine. I'll let him know you asked after him."

"Shit." Toby's voice was wry, but there was a thread of pain in it. Jared wished again he was there to put an arm around him. The best way to reassure Toby was through touch, along with words and tone of voice.

"Did you really take a swim this late?" He couldn't help the disapproval in his voice. He didn't like the idea of Toby swimming on his own in the inky darkness near the wharf; there were all kinds of ropes and anchors and other debris and he could get into real trouble with no one around to help him out.

"No," Toby confessed.

"Not feeling too good?"

Toby cleared his throat again and Jared thought he might be fighting tears. "No. Please, Jared, can you distract me?"

"Turns out I need distraction too. I miss you so much." *I haven't slept with Jai. If I had, I wouldn't be so fucking horny. I wouldn't be calling you in the middle of the night. But I'll let you work that out for yourself.*

"I miss you too." Toby sounded completely depressed.

"Let's set the scene, shall we?" Jared suggested, deciding to do what he could for Toby. His actor's voice was a powerful tool. He'd been able to whisper lovers in the past into coming without his touch, just from sound and inflection. Now he used it like a blanket, wrapping it around Toby to keep him warm.

"What do you have in mind, more incense?" Toby teased him.

"Are you questioning my authority, boy?" he asked in a silky tone.

"No."

"That's good. I'd hate to start off seeing you again with some kind of discipline, such as denying you sexual relief."

"I thought discipline would be spanking." Slight amusement lighting Toby's voice.

"Come *on.*"

"Yeah, I guess I like it when you do that."

"I guess you do."

He could almost hear Toby's thoughts racing, curiosity, and a little trepidation. But the depression was blowing off now, like mist over the water.

"What do you want me to do, Jared?"

"That's more like it," Jared approved. "I want you to find the lavender candles I store in the great room. Can you do that?"

"I think so. You keep them in that rosewood tiki cabinet, right?"

So Toby had been exploring. Jared smirked. He'd been expecting it. And it was such a lover thing to do, to be curious. He decided he liked it, though he would keep it to himself. He wanted to retain a little mystery, a little control, to stir the sexual pot simmering between them.

"Lavender is calming, a mood lifter. I want you to also mix some of the tangerine oil from the same drawer with the potpourri I have scattered around the room. That's energizing."

"I can talk to you while I do it," Toby said, obviously not wanting to break the connection. Well, that was fine since Jared didn't want to break it either.

"Okay." Jared bit his lip, wondering if he should ask the next thing that popped to mind. It was definitely a lover's question. Would Toby be up to that kind of thing? But his voice deepened as he asked anyway. "What are you wearing, Toby? Another of those fucking sexy black thongs?"

"That's such a clichéd question, Jared." But Toby's voice was smiling.

"Tell me anyway."

"A black silk robe I borrowed from your closet: the one with the red and gold dragon on the back."

It had been a gift from Jai. The little minx! But then he'd probably guessed the source since Jared had confided that Jai had something to do with his tattoo. Toby's interest and possessiveness was maybe a good sign though. Maybe this thing between them, that neither of them really understood but had obviously been simmering for the two years they'd known each other—maybe they really had a shot at being together.

"What else?"

"Yeah, okay, a black thong. I don't usually wear shit like that, but you seem to like it."

Jared groaned, making his way back to the guest room. He wasn't going to get through this phone call without stroking his erection, without giving into the need for relief. He just hoped that Toby was ready for that.

"Tease."

"I let the robe slip off and now I'm lighting the candles in just the thong."

"You're lighting more than the candles, little one. By the way, did you find my lighter?" Jared used a barbeque lighter for all his candles and incense to save time. He kept it in the same tiki chest as his other supplies. Had Toby found it and guessed what it was for?

"Yes, you control freak."

"So I'm a little bossy, but you like it." Again his tone was silky. The conversation had moved from the sharing of mutual desolation to sexual and so far it didn't seem to be scaring Toby.

"I like it a lot," Toby admitted. "I wish sometimes I didn't."

Jared frowned, not liking the sound of that. "Are you having any hangover from playing the role of my lover for real?" Damn, he wished he hadn't left right after they'd played. He should have stayed and made sure Toby was okay. But if he had, he would have lost his head and would have gone even deeper with him. He rubbed his forehead, wishing it were easier to find their path.

"No, I liked it. Too much."

"I don't think that you can like something too much, unless it's chocolate."

"I wish you were holding me so I could just disappear."

"Hey, that's not what I want, and that's also not what I thought you wanted." Again, there was the feeling of a wrong note. What was the source of Toby's sudden pain? He'd seemed grounded when Jared had left. "When I hold you, I want to see you, look into your eyes. It's a huge fucking deal for me, Toby. It's a privilege."

"Yeah?" The light of hope in Toby's voice. He thrived on being told he was good at something, that he was special. Jared had seen that as soon as they worked together on the soap.

Thinking about that now, Jared realized he'd been seducing Toby for a long time, not expecting anything would come of it, but instinctively giving him what he needed to blossom as an actor and as Jared's best friend. It wasn't like it was a chore; Toby was a very talented person, and Jared loved guiding him to acknowledge that. He could see that his own natural protectiveness; his sexual and romantic yearning for Toby had meant he'd been playing his boyfriend for real for a long time. No wonder Toby had turned to him! The last piece of the puzzle was sharing their bodies. Maybe they weren't as far apart as Jared had believed?

"Have you lit the candles?"

"Most of them. And I mixed the potpourri. It's nice, Jared. I love your home. I hope you don't regret allowing me to stay here."

Again, he heard that catch in Toby's voice. "Of course I won't. I'm not sure I could have left you at that juncture if I hadn't had the comfort of knowing you were still safely under my roof."

"Juncture. You mean what happened between us."

Jared settled deeper into the cool linen sheets of Jai's exquisite canopy bed, kept for the comfort of his guests. "Do you want to talk about it?"

"I didn't do it right."

"There isn't a right way, Toby," Jared said gently, glad to have the opportunity to talk about this now. "Your surrender was beautiful. God, you were so sexy, baby. Do you know how hard it was to leave you?"

"I thought you'd go there and Jai would tell you how you were better off without me."

Jared laughed. "If he did, I'm not sure I would listen to him."

"No?" Toby sounded wistful.

"No. I'm lying here hard and aching, thinking of you, baby. I wish I could see your face, touch your hair."

"That would be... nice."

"Does it freak you out when I tell you how much I want you?"

"A little, but it also makes me feel so good. Fuck, I'm a mess."

"It's a change."

"Yeah, you have a dick."

"I'm touching it now," Jared admitted mischievously. "If I was home and we'd been together a long time...."

"What?" Toby was settling down as well, Jared could tell. Maybe on the couch? That was a good place, with a view of the water and all of Jared's artistic touches. He wanted to guide them through their first phone sex if Toby was ready. He guessed he'd find out soon enough.

"I have a sling. Do you know what that is?"

"I saw a picture of it on one of the sites I visited."

"Intimidated you a little?"

"Yeah," Toby breathed, relief in his tone. "But it also made me curious. You know?"

"I do."

"Have you ever been in one?" Toby asked.

"Yes. Everything I want to do to you, I've experienced myself. I have some rings on the ceiling in the great room. They're discreetly covered by a panel, of course."

"Of course they are." Jared could hear Toby moving around, probably looking for the cut out. "Shit, that's been there all the time and I never knew!"

"Mmmmm. My secret self."

"So you'd put me into the sling?"

"My fantasy is having a gathering, just a few friends I've played with before. You'd be wearing something special I'd design for you, a piece of jewelry. I prefer to be discreet, so only you and I would know what it means."

"You've thought about that?" Toby's voice was surprised. "Pretty serious commitment."

"Toby, I have a confession to make; I thought about you all the time as my lover. I knew it would never happen, but it just seemed so natural I couldn't help myself. It's why I had to go away so often, to regain my perspective."

"Like how it is when we're together," Toby mused. "Natural."

"Yes," Jared agreed, thinking he'd come up here all this way to talk to Jai, but maybe he should have been talking to his new boyfriend. "Baby, I'd love to put you in a sling. Do you want to hear how it would play out?"

Chapter 9

JARED settled back on the bed, feeling better than he had since he'd left Toby after just a few moments of sharing with him on the phone. He was so deeply connected to him, the ties of need running between them, making him was just as vulnerable as his innocent boyfriend.

As he rubbed his forehead, listening to the rustling sounds carried over the phone, Toby no doubt searching for more candles, Jared felt the question he'd come all the way up here to ask of Jai caught in his throat. He also suspected the truth would not be something he wanted to hear.

If I give myself to Toby, will that mean that he'll one day reciprocate my feelings?

"Toby, have you by any chance had a visitor?" he asked, deciding to leave the car wreck of where this relationship was going and take what he could get.

"Visitor?" Toby's voice cracked.

"Yes, I asked Sahara Blue to come by and, uh, check on you."

He could almost see Toby blink, taking that in. "Sahara." He was a mysterious and soft spoken ex-Navy SEAL who looked like a surfer dude with an unusual seventies name. He lived in the houseboat across the pier from Jared's place. He had white blond hair, typically crusty with salt, because he was always in the water, and he had vivid blue eyes that always seemed to be restlessly scanning the horizon. He always wore a distinctive square pendant of shimmering blue beads the same color of his eyes around his neck—it was kind of disco, but tasteful disco. Toby had worked out with him and Jared sometimes. Jared had tried to talk him into being an extra on the show, but Sahara was too reticent about taking his clothes off. He had a particular hang up about showing off his back to anyone. Toby had a sudden hunch. "He's...? Wow."

"Gay, yes." Jared cleared his throat. "He sometimes assists me with exploring more elaborate erotic scenes; I've been trying to help him build his dating confidence."

"Another bird under your wing, Jared?"

"He knows that I'm concerned about you." Jared's voice tightened as he remembered a recent evening when, after too many beers shared with Sahara, Jared had gotten pretty emotional about Toby. Sahara had put him to bed, staying and rubbing Jared's back until he finally fell asleep.

"Someone else who knows all about your world."

"Toby, don't go there," Jared warned, knowing Toby wanted to know if he and Sahara had been intimate. "And I thought you wanted into my world."

"I just want...." Toby's voice dried up.

"What?" He felt the aching void between them and wondered if he pressed close to Toby in public again if he would shrink back, self conscious of Jared's touch. Probably. Shit, there was no way this could work. Jared had never had a boyfriend who wasn't comfortable with himself.

"Jared, I want *you.*"

"I want you too." Jared sighed. "But I don't know how to make that happen. I'm afraid this is a mirage, just something shimmering over the water."

"Is that why you ran away?"

"I didn't." Jared took a deep breath. "Maybe I did, a little. I want you too much, Toby. It clouds my better judgment."

"So Jai told you to dump me, didn't he?"

"No."

"What did he say?"

"Not much. We meditated."

"Meditated? Shit, you went all the way up there to commune with Buddha?" There was amusement in Toby's voice now. Teasing. Then he said, "Someone's at the door, so I'll call you back in a sec." There was the muffled sound of bare feet on hardwood floors and then he heard Toby greeting someone before Toby cut the call. Sahara Blue, probably. Jared's shoulders relaxed, thinking someone he trusted was looking in on Toby. He'd had a nagging bad feeling all day.

FEELING guilty as shit, because after what he'd done with Anita he had no right to be jealous of the mysterious Jai and now of Sahara, who had always seemed a sweet, timid guy, happy to be in Jared's shadow, Toby opened the glass heron door.

He swallowed thickly as he took in the handsome blond, having to remind himself again about that he had no right to feel possessive of Jared. It was weird this shy young man had ever been one of the legendary SEALs, and yet, maybe not. He did like to blend into the scenery, watchful behind smoky sunglasses.

"Hi," Sahara said softly. He gave Toby a swift look, as if gauging him, and Toby wondered if he'd call Jared back later and fill him in. The idea aroused mixed feelings in Toby. He liked Jared's protective side, but he wasn't sure if he wanted his vulnerabilities exposed to Sahara.

Looking at him wearing a body hugging black spandex vest and black swim bottoms—still dusty with sand, his body thin and cut like that of a perfect model, with prominent hungry bones, large eyes, pouty lips—just how had Jared resisted this guy? The answer was that probably he hadn't.

Depressed, Toby recalled all the men he'd seen in Jared's place over the years. He had been blissfully oblivious back then, but obviously they were men confident about their sexuality. Men who were comfortable being with other men.

Nothing like Toby, the fucking basket case. He couldn't even let Jared please him completely, and when Jared had snuggled close outdoors it had totally freaked Toby out.

He took a deep breath. Okay, it wasn't helping, brooding about this now. Jared had wanted him to call him back, so he redialed.

"Toby." Jared's voice drifted after he answered the call in one ring. Toby had the impression Jared wanted to ask him something. "Sahara's there?"

"Yes." Toby's voice softened. Jared made him feel like if he only surrendered, he would be pleasured beyond his wildest imaginings, safe in Jared's care.

"Remember that homework I told you about?" Jared's voice deepened. "About doing something so that you could take a cock inside you?"

Toby flushed and his gaze flew to Sahara, but the guy was standing at the great room windows facing the water, as if tacitly giving Jared and Toby the privacy to talk.

"If you go in my bedroom and look in my toy drawer—you remember where that is, right?"

"As if I could forget!" Toby padded toward Jared's bedroom, trying not to see the beautifully made bed with clean sheets as the betrayal it was. He ignored Sahara, leaving him in the other room, still trying to deal with his feelings for him. Shit, it had been so much easier when he'd been innocent of the subtext brewing between himself and Jared! He'd just thought Sahara was a nice guy. He hadn't even recognized he was gay, which went to show how aware he was of Jared's world, despite playing a gay character on TV.

He opened the drawer and took a moment to appreciate how organized it was. The tools, some of which he recognized from visiting sites on the Internet, were neatly organized. Gleaming pewter, flowing glass, and—

At the very top he saw what he guessed Jared had left him to find.

"A rectal dilator kit... Jared, this looks as exciting as braces," Toby said in an undertone, embarrassed that Sahara might overhear.

"I want you ready for me. Don't you want that, baby?"

Forgetting for a moment this was hopeless because of his mistake, Toby said, "Yes, I want to know what you feel like, just once." Toby swallowed, thinking it might be all he'd ever have.

"Remember I mentioned the sling?"

"Not likely to forget," Toby said wryly.

"I'm training Sahara to be comfortable with his need to dominate."

Toby's eyes widened. "*He's* like you?"

"One of us shy, under the radar types who has a secret side, yes, but he's a bit repressed. Probably one day some wild, irresistible man will make his life interesting and drag him out of his cave."

"Like I did you?" Toby smiled at the idea. "I didn't know you were shy."

"With the right person. It's all about wanting to please him."

"But you please me," Toby confessed impulsively, wanting Jared to know. He'd earned that with his gentleness, his control.

"Thank you, baby," Jared said softly, pleasure at Toby's spontaneous compliment in his tone. "Now where Sahara comes in is that I sometimes have him assist me with a scene. So he would be the one to help you into the sling."

Despite his mixed feelings about enticing and timid Sahara, Toby caught his breath. "He'd touch me in your place?"

"If you were comfortable with that. I have a big kink for playing the role of a kind of gentle Pasha to my lovers. I like making use of an assistant, and the trade-off is also good for Sahara, since he gains experience and is slowly becoming more comfortable."

"So you had to go through this process once, becoming comfortable with this side of yourself?"

"Absolutely. And for me it wasn't formulized. It didn't really gel until I was able to combine my spiritual beliefs with my kinky side."

Toby glanced at Kwan Yin, smiling sadly and mysteriously in a corner of Jared's room. He couldn't help remembering how the statue had been here when he'd given into Anita, like always, even when part of him had been screaming that this wasn't what he wanted, who he was anymore.

But having talked to Jared, he felt oddly like some of the goddesses' compassion and understanding had been given to him. He'd only just broken up with Anita. He'd only just given into his feelings for Jared, and that hadn't been easy. Maybe…what happened had been inevitable?

He chewed his lip again, wondering for the first time if it was really necessary to tell Jared what had happened here. It was sure to only hurt him, and the thought made a dull ache tighten in Toby's chest. More than anything, he didn't want to hurt Jared.

Maybe he could talk to Anita, bargain with her somehow. Protect Jared from the truth.

"You didn't just ask Sahara here to see how I was doing, did you?" Toby asked on a hunch, his voice warm and raspy to his own ears. Dimly, he had an idea of Jared's intentions.

"No, I wanted to ask you if he could… assist you with the dilator plugs," Jared admitted. "You said you didn't quite get the full effect from the other toy you used, so…"

Even though he'd had his suspicions, hearing it put into words was like a punch to the chest. "Shit!"

"I know. If I'm pushing, Toby, forget it, please. It's just my fantasy and I—"

Remembering how he'd let Jared down, Toby swallowed tightly. But maybe intimacy with Sahara was easier in some weird way. This wasn't Jared. This didn't pack the same emotional dynamite for Toby. "I'll do it."

"Toby?"

"I know what you're thinking, Jared, but I'm not doing this just for you. I, uh…." Could he admit it, even to himself? "It's not him, though. Do you understand? It's because I want to share your fantasy."

"YOU mean that you can see he is my... surrogate," Jared said, shoving back his hair. Fuck! This wasn't easy, exposing some of the ways he played to Toby. He wanted to cushion him, to hide this part of himself, but his heart told him he had to be honest or it would be unfair to both of them. They couldn't build anything real if it was constructed with an image he thought Toby could accept. He'd have to take the far more chancy route and ask Toby if he could accept Jared for who he truly was.

"Yeah. I guess it's not unlike someone standing in while I read my half of a conversation," Toby said, and Jared smiled at the idea of putting it into the perspective of filming the soap. Often Jared had done that with Toby, coaching him along. Toby always responded better to Jared than an extra filling in.

"It's a lot more personal than that, as I think you know," Jared warned gently. "Look, we don't have to do this now or ever. I really did want Sahara to look in on you. I was worried."

"Nothing to be worried about," Toby said lightly after a pause. "You're such a mother hen."

"I'm a mother something," Jared said.

"If you're focused on me, at least it means you aren't sleeping with Jai," Toby said. Then, "Shit, I didn't mean to say that!"

"I'm glad you did. Toby, Jai and I are probably going to do some Tai Chi in the morning, but that's all we'll do this trip, I promise you."

Toby let out a deep breath. "Thanks. I know it's weird. We're best friends, but all of a sudden any guy who goes near you, I think he's going to take you away from me."

"Sounds like you're feeling insecure." Jared got up from the bed and lifted his laptop onto it, booting it up. He'd need it for what they'd be doing next.

"On all counts. Remember how miserably I acted the first times on *Mission Bay?*"

The initial scenes between their characters had required them to fake having sex on a couch, Toby sitting on Jared's lap, his legs spread, Jared's palms spread over his bare ass.

And Jared had gotten hard. How could he not with sweet, confused, mortified Toby pretending to ride his cock? Teaching him how to kiss another man, to avoid getting beard burn. He remembered that lesson had made Toby laugh, since they were both unshaven to give the impression of a rumpled morning after.

Toby had stumbled woodenly through his lines and then Jared had taken him aside, suggesting he give him a massage and they talk for a while. Slowly that had relaxed Toby enough so he could give himself on camera.

Now remembering, Jared's eyes widened. Shit, way to seduce his co-star! He hadn't consciously thought of it back then, but that was a similar approach to gently wooing a virgin, not that Jared had ever had one.

Until now.

"Sahara will know how to make it good for you, baby. Will you trust me on this? I've worked with him often doing scenes, and he is very capable and gifted."

"What if he excites me?" Toby asked in a hushed voice. Jared could picture Toby's face scrunching up.

"I hope he does," Jared purred, finding the thought arousing. "But in this experiment, he really is just an extension of my will and my touch, servicing us both. His actions will give us both pleasure, and I can be sure he'll insert the device in a way that you should probably enjoy."

"So as a gay man you're never faithful to one person?"

"I..." Jared licked his lips. "I've never had a loving boyfriend. I don't know. But this isn't really the same thing. This is a scene that we talk about, that we experiment with. If it doesn't work out, you know your safe word, and I'll make sure Sahara does too. I'll be with you through the entire experience, watching over you."

"Jared, I want to take you inside me," Toby's voice was a thread. "If I do that...."

"If you do that, hopefully we'll both enjoy it. It doesn't have to mean more than that," Jared told Toby, told himself. Mastering Toby wouldn't mean forever, as much as Jared wished it would.

Chapter 10

TOBY found Sahara Blue kneeling in the great room. He was gathering some incense and as Toby hesitated, he asked in his light, sweet voice, "Jared told you?"

Toby scowled, trying to strangle more jealousy. "He ran this idea by you before talking to *me*?"

Sahara looked over his shoulder at Toby, white blond hair swinging into his eyes. "Nope, I just know him pretty well."

Toby gave a shrug. He had no right, but it made him insecure that Jared had Sahara and Jai.

"Toby." Sahara sighed. "The man is crazy about you, his unattainable, sweet Toby. Do you think any of us stand a chance with him? I wish...."

Toby's head fell back. Softly, "I'm just so insecure right now. It seems like I've been drifting toward him. To wanting to be more than a friend, but this is a direction I never thought I'd take, so how can that work? I know nothing about Jared's world. I mean, I didn't even know you were gay." Faint color touched Sahara's tanned cheeks. He lowered his eyes demurely. Huh, he sure didn't give off Jared's quiet cologne-ad confidence. "So how do we do, uh, this?"

"I need to speak to Jared. I assume he told you about the cameras."

Toby blinked and then felt his breath hitch at the thought. Oh shit. "No."

"Oh, he has them in his bedroom and the great room; some guy from your soap put them up for him, I think."

"He's been filming me?" Toby wet his lips. What if... God! What if the damn thing had been running while he'd been with Anita? Holy fuck! If Jared saw that, it would kill him!

"Not without telling you first," Sahara reassured, shaking his head. "Jared is always very direct about what he wants to do, very honest."

"So how many of these scenes have you done with him?" Toby asked, deeply relieved as he watched Sahara climbed to his feet and hold his gaze, as if considering his words. Not an impulsive guy, Sahara. Maybe this was the repression Jared mentioned?

"I've done a few scenes, yes." Sahara shrugged, long eyelashes shielding his eyes. He was still blushing, Toby noticed, amazed. Then the blue eyes lifted, the same color as the glittery square patch of azure beads worn around Sahara's neck. When those eyes held Toby's gaze, Toby experienced a twist to his gut.

As if reading Toby's confusion, Sahara nodded. "It's a little freaky, confronting yourself, what turns you on."

"You found it weird too?"

"Oh yeah. I, uh...." Sahara shrugged and unzipped his wet suit top.

As Toby stared, he realized that he'd never seen the other man shirtless. When Sahara turned around, revealing his back, he saw why. "Oh." He reached out, grazed a fingertip on Sahara's shoulder. "From when you were a SEAL?"

Sahara tugged the vest back on. "Yeah." He held out his palm. "Can we do this together, Toby?"

Toby's hand rose but then fell before he made contact. He just... he couldn't. Only from Jared could he accept this brand of comfort. Only in Jared's arms, with Jared's soothing purr in his ear did he feel sexy and safe and... loved.

"We can do this," Toby said. "But there are boundaries, so don't push them."

"Damn," Sahara muttered, but his eyes were lit with a rueful kind of amusement. "You are definitely a one man guy."

"I belong to Jared," Toby agreed automatically but then his eyes widened at how natural it was to say that. "I mean, it's weird, but he was always so protective as a friend, and I liked it. Now I want to do something special for him."

"I wish I had someone who would go to those lengths for me," Sahara noted wistfully.

"There's no one?"

"I have trouble letting anyone close." Sahara shrugged. "I go out, surf, run, do my bodyguard thing and also put in a little time as a lifeguard, but then I come home and live most of my life online. It's safer, man."

"An ex-Navy SEAL who likes it safe?"

"That's something else." Sahara's face hardened, and his eyes were cool, the eyes of a man who had been and done things Toby couldn't imagine, but just as quickly, the stranger was gone, like Sahara had covered a flame. "Hooking up with someone isn't easy."

"Anyone intriguing online?" Toby asked, raising a brow.

Sahara coughed, shaking his head shyly. He obviously didn't want to talk about it.

Remembering the scars on his back the other man had revealed, Toby nodded, understanding why even someone so good looking would be gun-shy. Then he chewed his lip, putting his hands in the pockets of his shorts. "What would make Jared really crazy?"

"A lot of things, but I know he doesn't want you to push yourself; he's extremely protective of you, even though I read you as a pretty stubborn guy."

"Huh, yeah, I am. I'm not sure I'm ready for too much either, so can you suggest mildly embarrassing, maybe?"

Sahara's brilliant blue eyes twinkled. "I could give you a shave."

"That's not embarrassing."

"It is where I'd give it to you." Sahara smirked.

JARED was pacing his bedroom, running his hands through his hair. He was too hot, too wired to sleep. He wished he could push his aching body against Toby's, to rub himself against his skin the way he'd wanted to all the time they'd been filming together. Two years of fucking torture! Not that Toby had meant to hurt him. He was just Toby. Sweet, fun to be around, comfortable with letting Jared throw an arm around him, although whenever Anita had shown up he'd pulled away, leaving Jared aching for what he knew would never happen.

Yet when he finally had what he'd yearned for, what had he done? Had he stayed with Toby, taken him, pleased him so he might not stray from Jared's bed? No. He'd run.

He closed his eyes, rubbing his bare chest in the spill of moonlight as he leaned against the open door and let the salt air stir through his hair, letting it calm him.

"Unrequited love sucks, huh?" Jai asked him, moving from the shadows. He tossed aside a herbal cigarette, and his gold and scarlet dragon tattoo seemed to writhe, alive and snarling, like a primitive arm band. His sleek body caught Jared's attention—he'd have to be dead not to feel it—but he looked away, remembering Toby's need for him to be faithful.

"Yeah, it really does." Jared took a deep breath, eyes stinging from more than the brisk night air.

Jai squeezed his shoulder. "I love someone," he confessed. "I have never told him."

"You could have anyone," Jared said, looking into his friend's tilted cinnamon brown eyes. How often had he feasted on those lips, let Jai take him, blow him away, leaving him gasping and sweaty on the bed in this house?

"It's just business with us," Jai said dismissively. "I have pulled away from him. You came up here to ask my advice on Toby?"

Jared nodded. "I asked Sahara to drop by and see how he was doing."

"You are extremely protective."

"I'm worried he'll go back to that bitch," Jared said baldly. Then he scratched his chin, rueful. "Shit, I know it's bad for me to feel this way about anyone. She's not such a bad person, I guess. She's just had the person I've wanted for years, and my gut keeps telling me she won't give up her hold on him easily."

"Hey, you're a spiritual person, I respect that, but you have a human heart. You are jealous."

"I think she's not what he needs."

"That is for Toby to decide, I think," Jai reproved gently.

Jared sighed. "Yeah. Goodnight, Jai."

Jai kissed his cheek, the brush of a butterfly, the silent reminder that before Toby and after, there would be Jai. He could lose himself in Jai's body, hold him down on the bed, and spend himself.

From what Jai had revealed, it wasn't like he'd have any objection. He was also wounded. What better remedy?

No wonder Jai was such a superlative courtesan, in the old fashioned sense of the word. He was like a chameleon, a mender of broken hearts and spirits.

"OH SHIT!"

"Come on, get into position."

Toby chewed his lip, a little more nervous now that Sahara had a razor and cool bowl of water. He was sitting on the edge of Jared's bed, legs spread wide, ass on a towel, blushing a fiery red as he exposed himself to Sahara and to Jared's camera.

"Any second now he's going to log onto his laptop and—"

"*Toby!*" The heat in Jared's voice, even though it was tinny coming through Sahara's laptop. Toby's gaze went to Jared's reflection, seeing the warm brown eyes wide and shocked, the lips parting. Jared groaned. "Oh baby, what you do to me."

Despite his nervousness, Toby felt an immediate lift. Jared desired him; Jared was pleasured by what he was doing for him. "It was Sahara's idea. He said you'd like smooth skin."

Jared leaned forward so the crude webcam on his computer picked up the hungry sheen in his eyes. "I'd love to rub my face between your legs, to suck your balls."

Toby's cock flexed and he laughed self consciously, his default to smile now that he was the center of Jared's admiration. It helped when droplets struck his skin, making him jump as Sahara spread him wide and carefully began to shave him.

He let his head fall back, feeling Jared's breathless attention focused on him, the object of desire; experiencing Sahara touching him, caring for him and when blue eyes caught his, he saw the buried need, the high color in Sahara's cheeks.

Being wanted translated into Toby running a hand over his suddenly sweaty chest, his nipples pebbling, his penis pulsing pleasure messages at every brush of Sahara's cool, capable fingers.

"Your boy is wanton," Sahara observed mildly as he gripped Toby's penis and held it aside for the undulating path of his razor.

Toby shuddered, belly dancing. So hard now, scared, lit up. If Jared were here, he'd want him to cover him, just put his large, muscled body on top of Toby's and pin him to the bed, thrust himself against Toby, let Toby rut against him....

"Jared," Toby murmured, feeling himself entering that weird, hypnotic mind space that he sometimes found himself falling into with Jared. It had only become more enhanced when Toby had chosen to surrender physically.

"Toby, so beautiful, baby. Do you know what it means, that you'd want to do something for me?"

"I'm going to itch when it grows back," Toby observed with a rueful quirk of his brow, but he felt that warm feeling in his chest expanding. Jared never failed to show him how he enjoyed Toby, thought he was smart, creative, *sexy.*

"Maybe I'll have my surrogate keep you smooth for me always, boy," Jared said. "Would you like that? Like it if he came by and cared for you while I watched?"

"As long as it meant we'd...." Toby gave a little shrug. "After." Sahara's touches, a servant preparing Toby for his master, only made Toby feel Jared's loss more keenly. If he were here, he'd fuck Toby.

His heart thudding, holding Jared's eyes, Toby knew it would happen just like that, that Jared would impatiently order Sahara from the room and then—

Sahara patted Toby dry gently, Toby laughing again, breathless because he was so fucking hard. Apparently he liked being the pasha's favorite, his body prepared for him, even as he wished like fuck Jared was here! He wanted Jared to come home to him. He wouldn't tell him about Anita; he'd handle that somehow. They just needed to be together.

"It's all right, I guess, but he's not you," he said, wanting Jared there so he could wrap himself around him like a vine, hide his flushed face even as he rutted against him. "I want my first time to be with you."

"Toby, if I were there, it wouldn't be much of a first time!" Jared growled. "Because I couldn't wait to be inside you."

Chapter 11

YOUR boy is wanton, Sahara Blue had noted in a calm voice, making Jared want to groan, making Toby chew his lip, uncertainty and heavy-lidded desire in his eyes.

He needs me. I need him. Color high in his cheeks, eyes riveted to Toby's, Jared reached out and touched the screen of his laptop, but the cool two-dimension wasn't what he needed. Couldn't be what Toby needed.

He lurched out of his chair, tearing his gaze away from the gut wrenching sight of Sahara urging Toby onto all fours, no doubt to shave him thoroughly. Oh fuck, did Jared ever need to watch that, but even more, he wanted to touch, to smooth a hand over Toby's back—

"*Jared.*" Jared started, looking up to see Jai's slight form filling his bedroom doorway. The normally serene man's brow was creased. "I felt unsettled energy under my roof."

Jared didn't question since he knew how sensitive Jai was, perhaps from all the meditation he did, all the work on raising his awareness. Instinctively needing to ground himself, he reached out and Jai clasped his hand firmly. "I... help me, Jai." He couldn't believe it, but his eyes stung. He was so raw, so vulnerable where his boy was concerned.

"It was a mistake for you to leave him right now while you're bonding yourself to him," Jai said, reading him accurately. "No, don't berate yourself; you didn't know. You were trying to do what is best for him. It was not fear for yourself that made you run, Jared. It was responsibility for Toby."

Chest moving rapidly, Jared parted his lips to speak but didn't have the words. Instead he released a sigh, experiencing absolution from the one person whose judgment he respected enough to accept it. He nodded. "It happened so fast! In many ways his girlfriend was his keeper, or it seemed that way to me, through jealous eyes."

Jai squeezed his shoulder. "You perhaps underestimated Toby's strength and resolve because the need between you is primal. I can feel that, a reflected heat coming from your body and heart." Humor moved in the sleepy brown eyes. "Like a car left out in the sun."

"I thought there would be some better way."

"You thought you could control what is largely uncontrollable. You can't spare Toby or yourself pain, Jared," Jai counseled, reminding Jared of how long Jai had spent in sanctuaries, striving to better himself. He combined the wisdom of a Buddhist monk with the arts of a courtesan. And even for him, there was pain, by his own admission.

"In fact, in saying this to you, that you can't avoid pain, that sometimes you have to follow your heart." Jai chewed his lip, robe slipping so that one cocoa nipple was revealed, his chest rippling with smooth skin over compact muscle. "I realize I am guilty of the same thing! I have tried to avoid pain. Perhaps I should begin dating again."

Jai looped his arms around Jared, smelling of sandalwood and patchouli, skin silken from the creams he used religiously. The familiar cool sturdy body soothed Jared, though his gut still twisted, the clang of *wrong* riding him.

"I will help you," Jai said, taking Jared's hand and leading him, docile, from his bedroom to the brink of Jai's room. "And maybe help myself at the same time. It's almost *dharma,* that I should do so. In turning away from truly living and letting someone in, I have turned away from myself, from the virtuous path."

"Jai." Jared paused, unsure of being alone with Jai in his bedroom. Jared had had to learn to divorce his yearning for Toby from his body's needs a while back, or he would have been a pathetic wreck, needing someone who could never be a lover. So he could lie down with Jai now, but for Toby's wishes.

Toby had an emotional need for fidelity. Jared could feel that, how Toby wanted that one rock in all the unsettled uncertainty he was experiencing right now. Toby had always been intensely loyal, fixed like the North Star in his affections; it was one of the reasons why he'd stayed so long with his girlfriend when to outsiders it seemed a relationship that had aged beyond its time.

Seeing Jared's distress, Jai reached up and cupped his cheek. "Trust me," he said softly. "You and your Toby have allies. Me, Sahara Blue."

Throat too tight to speak since he could almost feel the soothing concern coming from Jai, Jared nodded. "Okay. What now?"

"CAN you get up on hands and knees? And face the camera since I think Jared wants to watch your face when I do the rest," Sahara Blue directed in his soft voice that nevertheless gave the impression to Toby of a silken whip just kissing his skin. Strange. Sahara Blue definitely exerted some kind of control, like iron sheathed in satin.

"Okay." Mouth dry, Toby shifted around, his skin feeling cool and alien, his cock hanging heavy between his legs so he knew that Jared must see it. Sahara was matter-of-fact as he handled Toby, but he could sense his closeted want.

The razor dipped in the water, and he caught the soft wind chime of droplets of water hitting the bowl. Sahara Blue opened him and Toby stiffened, his cheeks burning. "Oh shit!"

"More than mildly embarrassing." There was a smile of amusement in Sahara Blue's voice.

"Um, yeah. You know what you're doing with that thing, right?" Toby couldn't imagine it would be comfortable having the equivalent of a paper cut *there*.

"Trust me; I've done this for Jared before."

Toby swallowed. "He has a lot of boyfriends, doesn't he?"

"Relax, boy." Sahara Blue smacked Toby's back lightly and Toby took a deep breath, trying not to jump at the soft rasp of the razor moving over his slick damp skin. "A lot of men want to take a holiday with Jared."

"Holiday?" Toby blinked.

"Jared is…." Sahara's voice tapered off. "It's hard to put into words, but you know you'll be cared for. He's extremely sensitive when mastering someone."

Mastered. Was that what Jared had been doing to him all along? He had fallen into this thing with him and it was weird, considering he probably should be on his own for a while after the break up with Anita, but this felt inevitable. It was like only being with Anita had kept him unaware, sheltered from Jared's pull, but when she pulled back, Jared was ascendant and Toby fell into his orbit.

A towel was pressed against his skin gently, Sahara dabbing him dry in some very private places. He'd seen Toby's ass. Touched it. Before him, only Jared had been so personal with Toby.

Toby noticed a figure of something drawn on the inside of Sahara Blue's left wrist. "A seashell?" he asked, referring to the tattoo.

"It symbolizes Aphrodite." Sahara Blue shrugged. "You know, Greek goddess of love. She came from the sea."

"You do spend a lot of time at the beach," Toby observed. "I guess that's natural for an ex-SEAL."

"When I was going through Hell Week, I thought I'd never want to go to the beach again." Sahara looked amused at the memory. "Now I can feel a part of something there but no one gets too close."

Then another detail struck Toby, who was hypersensitive right now; Jared had been pretty quiet during this last shave job. Had Toby done something wrong again?

"Jared?" he whispered. He looked over his shoulder, on his hands and knees, his body washed and shaved intimately by Sahara Blue—

The screen on the laptop was blank.

"DO YOU like grilled yellow pepper?" Sahara Blue asked him an hour later as he bent over the fry pan he had sizzling over Jared's old fashioned *hibachi* barbeque on the deck above his home.

"I…" *don't care.* But he couldn't say that, could he? He'd wanted Sahara Blue to take off and leave him alone, but the other guy seemed really worried about him.

What made it worse was Toby had seen bewilderment in his serene blue eyes, as if he couldn't understand why Jared had broken off contact during such an intimate shared act.

Rejected. Clearly something was wrong with him! He couldn't hold Jared's attention. Twice now after they'd been closer than Toby had ever been to *anyone,* Jared had pulled away.

This time he couldn't figure out what mistake he'd made, because he'd let Sahara shave him thoroughly. The other man had even taken time to praise him in the aftermath of Jared's desertion, but it hadn't done anything for the dull ache that lived in Toby's chest.

Jared. He needed him.

"I don't really care," he admitted, feeling totally shitty. Like eating was going to do anything. Why couldn't he have the stable and loving relationship he ached for? He'd always wanted to be with one person, to give himself, to get it right.

Sahara took a deep breath and handed him a Corona, as if he were resisting the impulse to express some kind of sympathy. Toby wanted to head downstairs into Jared's house, open Jared's closet door and sip his beer quietly in the near darkness where no one could see him and what a total fuck up he was.

He took a deep gulp of the beer to burn away the tightness in his throat. Jared had always been the one to comfort him in the past, but since Toby had pushed him into this wild experiment, it was Jared who hurt him.

A sudden dull sound woke Toby hours later. He was laying on Jared's bed, fully clothed, his skin still crusty from the salty dip he'd taken with Sahara Blue after their barbeque. He'd finally convinced the other man to leave him alone, though Sahara had made it clear he intended to stop by first thing in the morning and make sure Toby was all right.

He sat up, reaching for the matches by the bed instead of the light for some reason. A second later the match burned and he saw Jared sitting on the edge of the bed, taking his shoes off, the flame reflected in his soft brown eyes.

"Shit," Toby muttered, putting the match to the lavender candle. His fingers brushed the Larimer stones that Jared had left him for comfort, like a magical talisman, and then he forced himself to look at his missing... what? Best friend? Boyfriend? Master?

"I'm sorry I woke you," Jared said softly. "You were deeply asleep."

"I just bet you are!" The bitter words were out before Toby could think better of it, but he'd never been able to hide what he was feeling. Not from Jared.

"Toby, I'm so sorry I left you."

Toby studied the other man, wrapping his arms tightly around himself. "How'd you get here so fast? I thought you and Jai were going to have breakfast, do Tai Chi or some shit?"

"One of Jai's clients lent his private jet service so I could get down here a little faster. And a friend of his is driving my car so I should have it later this"—Jared rubbed his eyes and looked at the luminescent face of his bedside clock—"morning."

"Uh huh." Toby swallowed, remembering everything he'd done, how he'd exposed himself to this man, literally.

Tentative, Jared inched closer to Toby, as if he couldn't stay away. He reached out and stroked Toby's hair. Toby allowed it, face stiff but his eyes stung. He wanted to scratch his mark into Jared's skin. He didn't feel nice or kind or accepting like a best friend.

Jared placed his palm over Toby's rapidly rising and falling chest, his head tilting in that way he had when he was reading Toby. "I'm so sorry," he whispered, his tone intimate, different from the one he'd used to comfort Toby in the past.

Toby frowned, trying to figure out what exactly the difference was, then his eyes widened. There was honey in the tone. It was the voice of a lover.

"I'm so sorry, little one," Jared said again and now somehow he was surrounding Toby, arms around Toby's stiff chilled body, lips brushing his temples, his cheek until they sought Toby's lips.

Toby's hands dug into Jared's shoulders. He wanted to bite the other man. He wanted to hit him.

Jared glanced his lips against Toby's and just like that, just like the match igniting seconds ago, something flared wild between them.

Toby twisted Jared's cable knit sweater in his hands, working it as his lips parted and Jared took him, capturing his mouth, only Toby was far from passive. His pride stung, he kissed back the way he'd been too shy to ever do before. Moaning, he clasped his hands around Jared's neck, and then Jared was on top of him, crushing him into the soft bed. Toby's legs wrapped around the other man instinctively, holding him fast.

"I missed you so fucking much!" Toby choked, but then he was drowning again, Jared's hand fisted in his hair, Jared's hardness rubbing against his own aching cock and his heart galloping a wild pagan beat of joy, of possessiveness, of stuff too deep-dark-down in his balls to have words.

"I know. I'm sorry, I'm sorry," Jared chanted, kissing Toby's neck, then back to his lips, as if finding them the most succulent of fruit, thirsty to taste. "God, I couldn't stay another moment away from you."

He pulled away and made a soft sound, touching a sensitive place on Toby's skin where they'd rubbed beard burn into each other's skin. "I don't have the strength to stay away from you. If this is wrong, this thing with us, you're going to have to tell me."

"Dork." But Toby's feelings were still in turmoil and he needed to know. "You didn't fuck him, did you?" He knew he didn't have the right to be jealous, but he was.

"No," Jared whispered.

Toby tugged Jared's hair. "*Good.* Sahara told me that sometimes you allow your men to get fucked by someone else while you watch, but your dick is mine."

"Toby."

Tug. "Your dick, your body is mine, Jared," Toby huffed.

Jared groaned. "I wasn't arguing with you, though I'm hoping to put the chastity belt on *you* sometime."

"You don't need to do that." But immediately guilt lashed Toby as he remembered what had happened beside Jared's bed.

He shoved it aside, ruthless. *I'll take care of it. He'll never be hurt.*

After making that fresh resolve, Toby relaxed into the bed now he knew that Jared had been faithful. He knew he didn't have the right, that they weren't truly boyfriends yet, but it mattered to Toby.

"I keep my promises. I didn't touch Jai."

Toby was abruptly conscious of his painfully engorged penis, of Jared's earnest eyes, of the breath they exchanged. "Jared, take me, fuck me," he demanded, hands going to Jared's ass and pulling him even closer. He liked to be covered by the other man. He liked the feel of his dick. He didn't have to guess how Jared was feeling; it was there, solid, unmistakable.

"Not yet. It would be…." Jared's head fell back. "Shit! Give me a moment." He jerked away from Toby, panting. As Toby watched, he reached for the light switch with trembling fingers.

"Why not?" Toby demanded, cranky. He needed to get off. Now!

"Because it wouldn't be the way I imagined it," Jared said primly. "I had all these ideas. You have no idea how often I thought about it."

Toby studied him, seeing the desire for some kind of ambiance. It was so Jared with his incense and his giving thanks to Kwan Yin. Even when Toby came over for pizza sometimes there would be hibiscus flowers floating in a bowl and lit candles and shit.

But enough was enough.

He took Jared's hand and put it over his dick. "Your boy needs you," he said, knowing they were words that would light up Jared.

Jared didn't answer. As Toby watched, lips parted, the other man tugged open his pants. Toby lifted up and then he was sitting there, shaved, the air feeling oddly extra cool against his exposed skin.

"Oh Christ!" One hand cupped Toby's hip, and then Jared's warm mouth was on him. "You are so hot like that, all clean for me."

"*Jared!*" Toby was bucking, on fire to come, so hot to come after being touched and explored and prepared for his man. He tried to push Jared away, not sure if he should—but he couldn't help it! Shit, he was going to go off like a—

"Come for me, boy," came Jared's soft growl. "I want your come down my throat."

Chapter 12

JARED brushed the hair off of Toby's forehead, the gesture speaking to Toby of somehow being that of a father with a child, a lover with his beloved, a master with his slave. All three things combined in the simple action, the touch, callused fingers cupping Toby's cheek, slanted, warm brown eyes holding Toby's so that the moment bloomed like a rose, whole.

Toby pushed his face deeper into Jared's hand, into his keeping and Jared's lips parted. "Damn!" he cursed softly. "Waking up with you today was the best morning ever."

Toby had to agree after the pain and confusion, the hot coming together in the night had been.... Shit! He didn't have words. It had been too basic, too primal, as if he and Jared were inevitably drawn, inevitably touched.

Now as he watched Jared take out an old-fashioned skeleton key and unlock the door on the second floor of a Victorian building which overlooked the harbor where Jared's floating home was located, he flashed to the night before.

Hot. Oh yeah. Painful. Needing. Then exploding, his come on Jared, Jared's come on him. Perfect.

"Can't we—together? I never have… in a guy's mouth," he'd told Jared. Color flagged his cheekbones at the admission. He'd never imagined letting a guy suck his cock, though he'd been importuned by both men and women for a long time, especially after he'd started on the gay soap. But he'd had a girlfriend, so that was that. Toby was

fiercely loyal, liking to belong to someone. If he gave his come to Jared now, came in his mouth, he'd be enslaved. He knew himself well enough to know he'd crave doing it over and over again so that his fantasies would revolve around giving his spend to his new lover.

Huffing, lips shiny from his attentions to Toby's erection, Jared rested his head against Toby's thigh. "Shit, baby! Give me a moment. You aren't the only one ready to go off like a Chinese firecracker." He pressed his erection against Toby's lower leg through his clothing so Toby could feel the very solid evidence.

Toby's eyes widened. "Really? Just from—?" His act of submission had pleased Jared?

"YEAH, *from seeing you shaved, touching your smooth body." Jared traced the paler, freshly revealed skin, the blue veins, somehow fragile on his Toby, making him conscious of how he'd screwed up. "Um, did I...? I have a vague memory that I didn't sign off before heading down here. Fuck, I couldn't think of anything after I saw Sahara Blue shaving you. It was like this band was wrapped around my skull, pulling tighter. Had to see you, get close, touch."*

"Sounds like one of those weird alien viruses that the original crew of Star Trek used to come down with," Toby joked, obviously trying for humor.

"Yeah, mine was the Toby-disease. I think it might be fatal. So you didn't notice that I, uh, kind of disappeared?"

Toby shrugged but his blue eyes slid away from Jared's direct gaze.

Jared cursed again. "I'm sorry, baby."

"It's okay."

"No, it's not. I fucked up as both any kind of Dom and as your boyfriend." Jared said, kissing Toby's thigh. "My only excuse is, that if your fantasy man suddenly wants you, and you never fucking thought it could ever happen—" His voice tightened. "People like me, we don't

get the Disney ending, you know? So you just live your life and don't expect it."

But now Toby sat up, his face flushing with obvious shy pleasure. "I'm your Disney ending, really?" Then he arched a brow, and Jared just knew his young lover was going to be a tease, which sent pleasure shivering down his back bone, making his balls tighten. Oh yeah, tease me, baby. "Yeah, I can't think why you'd think I want you," Toby drawled.

Jared flushed, taking in Toby's evidence, his penis plum-colored at the tip, swollen, beautiful. That one look and he couldn't resist reaching out to touch, running a finger down Toby's length. "God, I love these," he growled. "I love to suck them, I love to torment them, I love them wrapped in leather and softening after coming. I love to hold one in my hand and hear my man begging to come and know he can only do it if I give my okay."

Toby gripped his wrist, panting, eyes glazed, his legs spread, wanton. "Jesus, Jared!"

"Close?" Jared whispered. "Are you close, baby?"

Toby nodded, licking his lips.

"Hurts a little?"

A more emphatic nod.

"Good. It's the good kind of pain."

Toby rolled his eyes and Jared laughed. "I want to try something. Will you let me try something to redeem myself as your prospective boyfriend?" Jared asked.

"Jared, Christ, do you think you're the only one to make a mistake?" Toby squeezed his eyes shut. He won't find out. In this very room, I took her, fucked her. He won't find out.

Jared leaned his forehead against Toby's, nuzzling. "You put yourself in my hands. Will you do it again, baby?"

"Yes," Toby whispered. Why not? He was Jared's plaything and the shameful thing was he got off on it. He didn't want to be seen kissing him in public, another man, would totally freak if Jared pushed

him to do that now, but in secret, he would let him do whatever he wanted.

"What's your safe word?"

"You forgot already?"

Smack! Jared slapped his hip and Toby's cock jumped. "Pistachio!"

"Good boy." Jared got up and went to his closet, stripping off his shirt, letting his pants fall as he did. His erection tented his boxers.

When he returned he had two leather belts curled in his hands. He uncoiled them, something about the movement suggestive.

And Toby tensed, eyes widening.

Jared squeezed his chin between two fingers. "Cute."

"You don't mean to...?"

"Naw." But Jared was fast, efficient. He put the belt around Toby's thigh, catching Toby's wrist so it was fixed in place against his leg. "Lie back. Relax."

"Okay." Toby swallowed thickly. His hand was tied to his thigh and that was a new one on him! When he looked down his body he was even more conscious of his cock, tumescent, needy.

Jared fastened Toby's other hand to his opposite leg and then opened a drawer, calmly taking out a package of condoms. It was the same package Toby had used with Anita. He swallowed at the guilty flash of memory and started when Jared rolled one on his cock, having lost the moment briefly. But he groaned at how thorough Jared was, stroking latex into place.

"It's a heavy-duty one. It should desensitize you slightly."

"Not very fucking much," Toby admitted ruefully. It occurred to him that Jared had tied his hands and now was putting his sex into bondage as well. The thought did nothing to cool him off. Color stung his cheeks.

"No, you're very sensitive," Jared said gravely. "You and I will have lots of fun with this." He ran a finger down Toby's cock, so obvious now, shameless.

"What are you going to—?" Jared sat on him, his legs on either side of Jared's legs, just below where he was tied. He reached out and took Toby's cock in his hand.

"Play with what's mine."

"Oh Jesus," Toby groaned, his penis reacting to measured touch, Jared's musician's calluses, the way he just took Toby's sex, handling it like he owned it.

"Like this?" Jared leaned down and Toby lifted up and they were kissing, despite Toby's willing confinement. His hands fisted against his legs, Jared's warm body pressing against his own exposed one, making him feel like a slut, like someone Jared had hired to tie up and display.

"I like you," Toby admitted. The graze of Jared's whiskers brushed against his own, and he felt the soft silk of warm, hungry lips, a tongue licking him like he couldn't get enough.

He needed Jared's guiding touch. He'd hated feeling as if his man was pushing him away even though it was so odd he had a man to begin with. God, what would his stepfather say if he ever found out? Toby swallowed, a little sick at the thought. He was such a coward, but he hoped Anita would keep her mouth shut. He wanted to be Jared's secret; alone with him, he could do what he wanted, be who he wanted, but he wasn't sure he could take it if people knew about them, or worse, knew about how Toby liked to be Jared's submissive lover.

Jared crawled down his body, his movement graceful, practiced and then as Toby watched, his attention riveted, tight, aching—

Jared nuzzled his sex and then took it deep, sucking it, settling in between Toby's legs like a man who planned to be there a while.

Sweat broke out on the back of Toby's neck and his forehead. It felt good, too good, even with the latex tightly confining him. Sexy, like his bound hands.

"Whore yourself for me, don't you?" Jared licked him.

"Yes, I do."

"I want to take a picture. I want that so that sometime when you are lying on my hardwood floor, nude, I'll place it where you can see it and be reminded of what you are."

"*No one will—?*"

"*I'll keep it safe. I'll destroy it if you ask me.*"

He'd never thought of allowing this, but the idea was a fucking turn on and this was Jared. Jared had always kept him safe. Jared loved him, protected him.

"*Okay,*" he agreed shyly.

"*Thank you, baby.*" He heard his sincerity. Jared picked up a small camera from the same drawer where the condoms had come from and reached out to spread Toby's legs, making his erection stand out even more prominently. "*Just the one for now, though sometime I'd love one with you wearing my come on your face, your tongue out, licking it from your lips.*"

Toby made a soft moaning sound, his throat tight.

Click. Click. The sound was as sexy as the links of handcuffs rattling together. It was sexy to think of Jared looking at the photo, wanting him, maybe lying alone in this bed when Toby wasn't with him and jerking off. It was sexy to think of Jared showing it to him.

"*Beautiful object,*" Jared whispered in his ear as he put aside the camera.

"*Jared!*"

"*Tell me what you want.*"

"*Suck it, take it. Please, Jared. Please suck my cock, God, I want to see you do it! I want to lie here, helpless, and see it in your mouth. I want to come and see it on your mouth—*"

Jared spread his thighs and took him as Toby begged and then Toby's hips were lifting and he was thrusting, clumsy, shallow, and he was inside a guy's mouth, his guy's mouth, and then he was coming, spilling, and Jared pulled away as lightning lit his nipples, his balls, his curled toes.

Huffing, Toby stared at Jared, wide eyed.

Jared freed him. Toby trembled, sensitized as Jared spoke softly to him, but in no time the comfort translated to…. Oh shit, he needed to be closer, to be covered, and somehow Jared was on top of him again, kissing, holding Toby's hips, cradling him, and Jared caught his wrists to hold him still as he slowly—slowly—thrust his silk covered cock against Toby's slick one.

He stared into Jared's eyes, caught as much as he had been when Jared had tied him. His breath suspended and released with every achingly slow thrust.

"Oh Toby, fuck!" His back arched, his cock pushing against Toby's body as Toby felt moisture saturate the cloth between them.

After, Jared and Toby lay in a drowsy heap, exhausted like puppies, sweat drying like lovers. "I feel like you're a vampire and you've sucked the life out of me," Toby rasped, stroking a hand over Jared's back slowly. A man, yes, and that still rang wrong, but his lover. Jared, his lover.

"I came in my boxers," Jared admitted in a foggy voice. "I should.... We need to.... Burn some incense and open the window and shower, and I have some new gel I'd love to use on your skin. Tastes like figs and chocolate. And I need to meditate."

His eyelashes brushed against Toby's chest as if he was listening to Toby's heart beating.

Toby stared at the guttering candle and felt exhaustion and contentment, felt like somehow this was all going to work out. "Go to sleep, you big geek," he ordered.

He felt Jared smile against his skin and then felt the kiss he pressed against Toby's heart.

SO TOBY was still glowing from their rebonding as they stood in the landing of the drafty building, and Jared opened the door and kissed Toby on the lips. "In this room you'll be mine." Part warning, part electricity.

"Like this morning?" Toby asked.

"More," Jared said.

Not knowing what to expect, Toby wet his lips, walking inside, and Jared whispered, "*Kneel.*"

Chapter 13

KNEEL.

The word was a silken whisper, a command, a suggestion gift wrapped over something primal.

Toby caught his breath and felt his legs give way; it was suddenly that easy. He looked up at Jared, who reached out and combed Toby's hair through an unsteady hand, eyes brimming with feeling: relief, love, desire, acceptance. "Good boy," he said. "Look around you."

Toby pulled his gaze from Jared's with difficulty, taking in a bare warehouse space, high ceilings, crumbling brick walls barely brushed with cracked ivory paint like a subterranean animal shedding its camouflage, and tall windows with the morning sun coming in, highlighting rectangles of battered hardwood. The room was absolutely empty except for a silently swaying heavy metal hook held from darkened chains which looked like they had served some kind of industrial purpose a century ago.

"What do you think?" Jared leaned against the wall, crossing his arms and watching Toby, as if prepared to stay there all day, as if he had nothing better to do and all his focus, all his attention were for Toby.

He is for me. I am for him.

Heart thudding in his throat, palms damp for some reason, Toby said, "Uh, empty."

"Yeah, it's a ring box," Jared noted, slanted brown eyes touching the details of the space as Toby had a moment before. "This is my favorite space."

Toby lifted his brows in inquiry.

"An empty box that serves as a show piece, a pedestal to display something precious." Jared was staring straight at Toby now.

Toby's heart gave a big *thump* in response. He licked dry lips and cleared his throat.

"Getting some ideas?" Jared asked, lifting a brow. His crossed arms emphasized his smooth skin in the pale blue T-shirt, olive colored with black hairs on the backs of his forearms, muscles discreetly undulating, muscles that Toby had traced with his tongue in a recent take for their soap. He remembered how Jared had held his gaze as he'd done it. Remembered the feel of the erection pressing against him as he sat on Jared, forgetting for the first time that this was supposed to be pretense. Was this what Jared had experienced all these months?

And was this also why Toby had found it so natural to turn to him as a lover? Kissing, touching, trusting. His pretend lover was slowly morphing into the real thing.

"Suggestive is the word of the day," Toby noted. "This is a place for me. I'm the only object in the room. I'm the precious thing."

"Very good. Strip." The second word caught Toby again. The same measured tone but the word *strip* full of power, seeming to echo extra large in his head, like the distant boom from a drum.

Self–consciously, he climbed to his feet, wiping his hands off on his jeans before tugging his own T-shirt off, eyes falling modestly. His penis was pushing against his pants; Jared's purring tone, the purpose of the room, being Jared's jewel du jour. Shit!

As he opened the buttons of his jeans, his fingers grazed the lumpy thing hidden in his left pocket. He almost smiled then, remembering what he had for Jared. When would he give it to him? He pictured it briefly. It was perfect for Jared, but it would have to wait.

The room demanded his attention now.

His jeans fell to his ankles and he took a deep breath, kicking them away, feeling oddly like he was removing more than his clothing.

He mulled over what Jared had meant by "this is my favorite space." Because here Jared could be himself?

The things he liked, the spiritual, the sexual—it had to be stuff he was probably no more eager to share with the world than Toby was to share his need to belong to Jared. It was strange to think of his quietly confident best friend as vulnerable.

Speaking of vulnerable, as he put his thumbs under his silk boxers, he felt it. His eyes darted up and met Jared's simmering ones, the emotion between them a punch to his chest.

This meant something. This wasn't just him shedding layers of clothing. This man was in love with him. To Jared, he was the sexiest, most desirable man in the world.

The thought steadied him and made heat flush his chest, neck and cheeks. He was Jared's precious object. The silk caught on the wet tip of his cock and Jared's lips parted, as if he wanted to get down on his knees and lick the taste from Toby's flesh.

Panting softly now, Toby let the soft material fall and then kicked it away emphatically, conscious of the extra silkiness of his body, still freshly shaved for Jared by Sahara Blue's thorough touch.

"Put your hands behind your back," Jared ordered softly.

Toby shivered, his balls tightening deliciously as he obeyed, wrapping one hand around his wrist.

He waited, breathless, wondering what Jared would do. There were no props in the room, not even a chest, a container, not even a chair. The only possession was Toby himself.

Jared walked past Toby and Toby caught the sound of the lock. *Snick.* Heart beating thick, hot, he waited. He was rewarded finally with the brush of fingers against the back of his clasped hand.

Jared's finger stroked the curve of Toby's bare ass and Toby jumped, laughing breathlessly. "Jesus!"

"Oh yeah, baby." Jared kissed the side of his neck, warm lips against cool skin. Toby's nipples peaked in response. His erection was unsubtle, aching, heavy, as if asking a question of his new lover. *I need to come. Will you let me come, Jared?*

Jared circled him and then unexpectedly dropped to his knees, doing it as easily as Toby had earlier. It was this world they shared. Broken away from who they were supposed to be, the skin they wore outside. Now they were both naked, though Jared still wore his T-shirt and jeans.

Jared reached into the front pocket of those jeans now, lifting free a couple of items: a small box of Japanese incense in the scent of autumn leaves, and some lotion.

"I wanted to do this first thing this morning, but we got that call to come in and do a retake," Jared admitted ruefully. They'd been groggy, sleeping like puppies pressed together, and then jolted by the summons, out of bed, in the shower, barely time for a kiss before they arrived on the set, sipping hot Starbucks and trying to put feeling into the two lines they had to share.

All the time Jared had looked at him, worked with him, the spice between them steaming like the coffee. Toby conscious that everything had changed between them; now they shared a secret. It was sexy, but it also made him break out in a cold sweat, thinking anyone might find out about it.

Jared spilled out lotion on his palms after putting the little box of incense aside. He warmed them and then reached up, hands making contact with the freshly shaven skin around Toby's penis.

"*Fuck!*" He was going to need to come. Soon!

Jared's slick fingers, callused, sensitive, exploring, gliding, the cool cream, Toby's wide shocked eyes holding Jared's as his man worked the cream into his skin. "This is for me, Toby," Jared said. "I want to touch you, find you smooth, push my face against you—" He leaned close and his lips brushed the stem of Toby's cock.

Toby's hands were in Jared's hair.

"Toby!" Jared smacked his hip. "I said put your hands behind your back." His voice was stern, reminding Toby he'd put himself into Jared's care.

Toby whispered, a little chagrined, a lot turned on, "I might—shit, Jared, I feel like I'm going to come. Without you even, you know, touching me!"

Jared smiled, nuzzling Toby's oily thigh. "Perfect."

JARED lit the incense, leaving the little black square by one windowsill so that scent drifted lazily in the drafty space. He stared out the window, contemplative, eyes closing briefly, so that Toby wondered if he were saying some kind of prayer to Kwan Yin or whatever.

It made tenderness and yearning crowd Toby's heart. What was it like to be so centered? Sahara Blue had said discovering your true nature was freaky.

After Jared finished his small ritual, he returned to the brick wall and leaned there in a square of warm sunshine. His eyes half closed, he watched Toby. Not telling him what to do, just... watching.

Toby swallowed, not sure what he was supposed to do. He paced the room, bare feet, super-conscious of his nudity, of his thudding heart, his hard prick wobbling between his legs. Embarrassment stung his cheeks at how obvious he was, how slutty, but at the same time he was excited by it. He felt like a whore on display for his customer, like a model ordered to pose for an artist, a boy bought to a pasha, his body to be enjoyed, watched, until—

He flashed to Jared and him at some future appointment here, him bent over one of the dusty windowsills, his legs spread, moving up and down as Jared thrust inside him, using him, fucking him.

His hand went to his cock.

"No, boy," Jared growled, finally saying something.

Shit! Toby clasped his hands again behind his back. Why was it so hard to do something so simple?

Then his attention, his axis shifted.

Jared's attention was fixed on him. He hadn't stopped watching Toby since they'd entered the room.

And now Toby looked to Jared. As soon as he held Jared's gaze, the other man's eyes softened, the brown light mellow in the sunshine. He gave a slight nod, as if he could read Toby like clear water, could see that he'd taken his first step through this new maze where he had chosen to lose himself with only Jared's guidance.

Holding Jared's eyes, Toby walked toward him, full circle, and as he did, he heard Jared's first words when he'd entered this space, *kneel.*

When Toby reached Jared, he slowly lowered himself in front of him, still caught in the eye fuck, lips parting, arms clasped obediently behind him.

On his knees, it felt easier, his focus not the whole room, not the future, not worrying about what might happen if they were ever caught together. Now it was just Jared.

Following instinct, Toby leaned forward and put his lips against the hard ridge of Jared's erection, covered by his softened jeans.

Jared breathed out a laugh, head falling back against the warmed brick, hands rising on either side of his body, fingers scrabbling over uneven texture. He didn't speak, didn't encourage or coach, but his body shouted to Toby.

Touch me. Please touch me, Toby, oh fuck!

Yin and yang. Wasn't that some of the shit that Jared was always talking about? He wore a pendant today with the simple white and black, two halves sliding silver between his pointed nipples.

Yin, giving.

Toby rubbed his cheek gently against Toby's hard encased prick, feeling his lover was in bondage as Toby was bound.

Suddenly impatient, he broke Jared's edict, using his hands so he could free Jared of his jeans, unbuttoning them as he held heated tan eyes, caressing the hard ridge, tugging down denim and cotton and then replacing his hands behind his back; *I'm your good boy.* Leaning forward, his pose striking him as reminiscent of a man worshiping at an altar, he took a deep breath and then Jared's cock was in his mouth, pressing warm and insistent and hard.

Jared gasped, his body shivering at the stroke of Toby's tongue.

"God, Jared, I want to suck your cock," Toby whispered, raw. "I want to be like this, just like this, day or night and I want you to push it in, fuck my mouth with it. How can I want this so much?"

Jared's eyes, sizzling now, like burnt honey. He laughed, as if buoyed by their secret world. "I want my come on my boy's face, just like I want my handprint on your ass."

"I'm not so straight, I don't think," Toby admitted, uneasiness rumbling under his breastbone, but this was Jared, he could admit it to him. "Maybe they were all right about me; Anita, my step-father. I mean, why else did I take a role as a gay man without even thinking about it twice unless—" Toby bit his lip. "Unless it was the only way I could live vicariously as the man I might have wanted to be, you know, in another life."

"You've been killing me since I met you," Jared admitted softly. "Killing me so I'd wake up, sweaty, hard, and no one, no beautiful man, could push you from my gut. I was crazy to have you, my best friend." He closed his eyes. "But if I touched you, you would have told me to go to hell and I couldn't take that. I was selfish for every part of you that you would give me. I set out to seduce you, if not physically, then I wanted you to confide in me, spend time with me."

"You were waiting for me," Toby said. "Somehow you were waiting for me."

"Yes," Jared admitted. "But Toby, I think part of me was always scheming, wishing. I wanted you away from *her*. I wanted you to be mine. If I could have willed you to come to me, I would have done it."

"Jared, it wasn't Jedi powers that brought me here," Toby confessed, throat tight. "You are my best friend. I trusted you enough to come to you, to bring these feelings to you."

Jared closed his eyes, swallowing hard so Toby could see he was finding it difficult to speak.

But maybe the time for talk had passed.

"You're my best friend," Toby whispered, kissing Jared's penis. Here he was, on his knees, the little cocksucker his stepfather had accused him of being often because of his easy nature. "And you're my master."

Jared sucked in air, groaning as Toby laved his slit, sucked the tip.

"And I want to be naked for you. I want to be in this room. I want to be on my knees." Toby's breath hitched, more than clothing falling away. "I just want to suck your cock."

Chapter 14

TOBY lost himself in texture, in scent.

Jared's bush was musky, crisp against his face as he brushed against it. His precum tasted salty, and in licking it, Toby heard the words of his stepfather again, derisive: *you little cocksucker.*

Words meant to hurt, to control, to humiliate. Even if he'd never given into temptation and tasted Jared, sucked him, would he always have secretly wondered how another man's cock would taste?

Now those words turned him on. Why was that? He couldn't explain, but the more he pushed back the curtain that separated his life from Jared's, the more he felt like he was writing on a new page, a page with his own words, feelings, not something that was expected of him.

This was the path he'd been warned to stay off. This is the path where he'd finally strayed. Because of Jared.

"I'm your...." He pulled back, lips shiny, eyes looking up at Jared who was panting, not at all remote and godlike and unmoved but hot, melting for Toby, desperate to come on Toby.

Jared seemed to read him, seemed to know what Toby had to say, to claim as his own. "Say it out loud."

"I'm your little cocksucker," Toby said all in one breath. He leaned his forehead against Jared's thigh, in a pose not unlike someone bowing to a superior. His blood was thumping in his own cock, excited, but he knew that it would only be Jared who could release him to finally come. Jared who was his guide in this scary and enticing new world.

"You're my beautiful cocksucker," Jared corrected, stroking Toby's hair. "I've dreamed of my cock in your mouth, of my come on you."

"Where?" Toby breathed, loving this closeness. He'd felt hollow when Jared was away. It probably wasn't PC, even thinking it, but he'd felt like a container, waiting to be opened, used. His cheeks flushed at the thought. But as much as he'd done what his family, what his girlfriend had wanted, he'd never gone along like this.

The reason was simple: this was what he wanted, at last.

"Boy, go sit under the hanging chain," Jared purred, his voice saying he was enjoying their game.

Blinking sleepily up at Jared, Toby complied, thinking it wasn't so different from when they were on camera. They had to put their hands, their lips and tongues and bodies in specific places for the angles of each shot. They had to make believe they were lovers, intense, knitted together, all while remembering it was just pretend. But he'd strayed. Jared's warm hand, Jared's soft voice, had led him from the path, had made this real.

On his ass in an oblong of sunshine, he felt oddly blessed. This wasn't some cold stagy place. It was just him and his new master. Their bodies. Their hot lust.

Jared used his foot to widen the separation between Toby's legs, holding his gaze as Toby looked back, his erection still sticking up, untouched, aching, and then Toby had a sense just how Jared intended to touch him.

He would mark him, mark his territory. Mark what was his now.

Jared kissed him, eyes on his lips and then he sat back, reached for a D ring that was recessed in the floor and opened it, revealing a small storage space.

Toby's curious gaze went to it immediately but Jared only smiled and pulled out a black silk scarf. He tugged it around Toby's face, covering his mouth, gagging him, before taking a moment to stroke his back, as if reading Toby's body language; his hand rested approving on Toby's thigh when he sat silent.

"You can't give me your safe word gagged, so if you want me to remove it, I want you to drum your feet, okay? I won't be restraining your legs."

Toby rolled his eyes, saying, *I'm fine.*

Jared frowned. "I know this seems building block simple to you right now, but if we decide to explore something more difficult for you to accept, I want you trained to let me know your limits."

Hearing Jared's concern, Toby nodded. *Yes, I understand.*

With his speech temporarily gone, Toby found he was open more to his surroundings, as he had been when Jared had covered his eyes previously; he was aware of the slight movement of the chains swaying above him. He was aware he was sitting in the glow of lemon light coming from outside and it made him feel protected, safe. When Jared took his wrists and he felt rope brush his skin, his breathing picked up as he anticipated what was to come.

What are you going to do with me?

"I'm tying your hands above your head, but I will leave them loose and I won't leave you in this position long, baby, or it'll be uncomfortable." Jared kissed him on the side of his face tenderly, with a vibe that said he was very much Toby's guardian.

Toby watched as Jared climbed to his feet, his hands pushing down his jeans then removing the T-shirt so he was as nude as Toby was. He penis stood out from his body and Toby's gaze riveted on it, thick and veined. He'd sucked it, the first man he'd ever sucked, and he would let Jared fuck him. Soon.

"Good boy," Jared whispered, as if knowing that if he wasn't gagged, Toby would accept Jared's prick in his mouth. He shook out more of the hand lotion he'd used on Toby earlier, rubbing his own cock, standing there touching himself while Toby watched, kneeling, bound, the only sound the slick, hot movement of Jared fisting himself.

Toby watched as Jared's throat corded and his head fell back. He looked incredibly hot to Toby now. Why had he been oblivious for so long to how sexy Jared was, how beautiful the simple lines of his sleek body?

He knelt behind Toby and Toby felt the wet, slippery feel of Jared's hot stiffness poke his lower back. He knew that Jared wanted to fuck him and he almost couldn't wait for the command to impale himself on Jared or to bend over on his stomach with his ass raised in invitation. What would it feel like to take a man's thick cock?

"Maybe the second time I fuck you, it would be during an unusual movie night at my house," Jared speculated softly.

Toby raised his eyebrows, encouraging Jared to continue as his lover rubbed his penis against Toby's back, his arms around him, his hand reaching between Toby's legs and claiming Toby's prick in his oily hand.

It felt....

Toby groaned, so hard it was close to pain. He couldn't help but sit up, his body at attention, craving every touch Jared would offer as he humped himself against Toby's bound body.

Jared kissed him, all the tenderness speaking of a boyfriend for his cherished one, his working of Toby, his slow fuck against his back making Toby's head fall back as he lit to every touch.

"It's the kind of movie night I used to fantasize about having you over for. Popcorn, action movies, beer, and you'd be like this, nude for me, sitting at my feet." Jared nuzzled him and Toby shuddered, giving a groan as Jared circled his cock head with a gentle finger. Toby immediately wanted Jared to do it again because it was the most amazing thing, like lightning that zapped his nipples, his ass, and his penis.

"I'd ask you, in the same tone I'd use to ask for a beer, for you to bend over my coffee table."

Sweat broke out on Toby's forehead. He was moaning constantly now, using his sound like a cat purring so Jared would know he loved to be handled.

"Do you know what I'd do then, Toby?" Jared tongued Toby's ear and Toby shuddered at the warm feeling, the tiny penetration and control. "I'd put my fingers in your ass with some lube, stretch you out, and then I'd unzip and make use of you right there in front of the other men and their boys. That would be the second time I'd fuck you."

Toby was shaking now, shaking all over like an aspen tree in a strong wind. He was going to come! He was going to go off like a fucking cannon, but he needed.... He moaned, and Jared took his prick firmly in hand, kissing him as Toby surrendered completely. "Good boy, cream in my hand now. You've been so good, so beautiful, Toby, and I want your come in my hand. I want my pet to come when I say."

Toby's body jerked and he grunted, coming just as Jared had ordered, a red band tightening around his skull, and then everything exploded, and he could feel Jared rutting against him, his embrace tight, loving, just what Toby needed, and then his relief splashed Toby's back and ass, his wet penis pressing against Toby, insistent, wanting inside him.

His Jared wrapped around him, loving, sweaty, eyes closed, Toby knew one day soon he would be inside him, and he ached for it.

"INTO the shower with you, boy," Jared ordered with mock harshness, but he was having trouble keeping the smile off his lips as he smacked Toby's hip.

Toby gave a laugh, obviously not very intimidated as he looped his arms around Jared's neck with a new assurance. Jared could see they'd found more in the bare warehouse space than he'd hoped for. More intimacy.

"Only if you come in there and wash my back and other parts." Toby was teasing, displaying the new assurance Jared had given him.

Jared leaned his forehead against Toby's, taking a deep breath because this was everything and more he'd ever dreamed of. The Disney moment, yeah. "I love you, Toby," he breathed.

"Jared." Toby stroked his cheek. He didn't give Jared an answer, but Jared wasn't sure he could have believed it, that Toby would ever come to love him back, considering he was just the first guy Toby had ever been with. But maybe they could be this close, friends with benefits. That he could accept, gladly. It was more than he'd ever thought he'd have.

"I'll be right in there," Jared promised. "I just need to get some fresh towels from the bedroom closet."

"Okay, I'll start the water running, but remember we don't have long on a houseboat," Toby advised. He dropped his robe and treated Jared to a flash of bare, enticing ass which he wiggled—the imp!—before disappearing into the bathroom.

"Brat!" Jared muttered. Toby was just asking to be tied up and played with until he begged in a low, husky voice.

Jared was still smiling as he entered his bedroom. He stared at the bed for a moment, still unmade from this morning which was out of character for Jared—he *always* made the bed after finishing with one of his encounters. But Toby was different. Besides, for some reason when he'd first returned, he'd sensed some reticence from Toby about sharing the bed with him, but maybe that was because it was another first, sharing a bed with another man.

What had he come in here for again? He was still lost in a haze of relaxation post-release, of the shy joy at feeling so close to Toby.

Towels, right. He had folded some recently and....

He frowned when he spotted a bright scrap of mauve poking out from under the bed. Something of Toby's? He bent down and picked it up and as he stared at it, turning it over in his hand blankly, everything changed.

Chapter 15

SAHARA BLUE shed his clothing as soon as he walked into his gently rocking floating house. One thing he'd always liked was to be nude. He felt primitive, in touch with his essential nature, but not vulnerable. His house was seeded with all kinds of things he could use to fight, to kill, and his bare hands alone were lethal.

He sighed, pushing away the cold, focused warrior part of himself. He was tired, so he rubbed gritty eyes, wanting nothing more than his bed for a few hours, but he was hooked by the idea that *he* might have posted again on his blog.

He'd gone to a seaside crab shack where sometimes he saw other cute guys he was almost sure were gay, but he hadn't worked up the courage to buy anyone a beer. Again. It was easier when Jared went with him because somehow he felt centered and not such a dork. All the time he'd been in the SEALs, he'd lived like a monk, so it had been his nickname with the guys. But the truth was, he'd burned every night to touch someone, to have someone.

But it hadn't happened tonight since he'd been alone and Jared was very focused on his own romance now. Knowing how long he'd ached for Toby, Sahara couldn't blame him, though he missed his friend.

But it was fucking hard trying to make a connection, to get close to anyone, when he was afraid of revealing his true self. Not just the scars on his back, but the desires of his body. He still struggled with feeling like a freak because everything about him from his weird name to his fondness for tying guys up made him feel different. The only intimacy he could risk was a quick stand up fuck in an alley, otherwise even the most casual guy might ask him why he couldn't touch Sahara's back and Sahara still couldn't bear anyone touching him there.

Which was also stupid; he took his wet suit vest off at the beach, so it wasn't like he wasn't used to people seeing his back. But that was another context where for some reason he didn't feel exposed.

He hovered near his small study, debating. Sometimes after reading some of the things Lotus posted about, Sahara found it seriously hard to sleep. He even dreamed now about the unknown and provocative man who shared exotic and sexy stories.

Yet, despite the hot narrative, photos, and intelligence of Lotus, what Sahara found touched him most was Lotus's unhappiness.

Sahara had given up, too, not that he'd ever had the courage to come out of his shell much, afraid of the ferocious passion under his impassive surface. Sometimes he cursed his own hidden nature, because he wasn't the perfect sexual match for Jared, not the yin energy that Jared talked about, but mostly yang.

After his dorky experiences trying to get close to someone, he found it hard to reveal himself, though Jared had told him that he was also a caregiver and finding a good match with someone who enjoyed that aspect of his personality would probably be healing and satisfying.

Lotus. How often had Sahara imagined what it would be like to have him in his home? He would start with sushi and progress to gentle bondage of some kind. Nothing too elaborate to try to impress, just the basics because he had a feeling that would be something Lotus would enjoy. And he wanted to give Lotus pleasure, to see the unknown man come alive, focus on an experience that only Sahara could offer him.

But what a loser, he hadn't even managed the courage all these months to leave a comment on Lotus's blog.

Sahara sighed, but, unable to resist, he booted up his laptop, clicking on the shortcuts that took him to Lotus's home page. He caught his breath when he saw a new picture of a man in a submissive pose, this time bound by what looked like rough hemp rope to a tree. The photo was grainy, as if taken by an amateur, and Sahara's fists clenched as he stared at the dark curly head of the naked man, turned away from the camera. He was familiar, as was the thick, semi-erect penis between his legs.

Sahara was almost sure this was a photograph of Lotus himself.

He reached out to touch the screen, not reading Lotus's comments about the picture, but putting his head over his folded arms. He'd been right; he wouldn't be getting much sleep tonight, thinking about Lotus and how he wished he'd been in the photograph with him, touching him.

"TOBY, you've changed your hair." Ellen smirked when Toby ducked his head, standing as she applied body makeup. Toby was a bit chagrined that so many of his scenes were in the nude. Kelly always seemed to be in bed with Aspen, but of course, that meant that he'd be in bed with Jared, so maybe it wasn't so bad.

And right now he needed to see Jared, who hadn't showered with him yesterday as they'd planned, much to his disappointment. He thought they'd been getting closer, but the other man had been quiet, barely meeting Toby's eyes after Toby left the shower and came to find him. Toby couldn't figure it out. They'd been laughing one moment and then…. His gut told him he'd done something wrong but Jared had denied it, just said he needed some time alone to meditate.

Aching, Toby had left Jared's home, after exchanging one intense glance with Jared through the barrier of the Heron glass door on his way out. He'd returned to his barren apartment, experiencing this weird feeling that Jared was locking him out of more than his home.

But why?

He'd gone over and over his time with Jared since he'd returned from visiting his friend Jai, but all he and Jared had done was kiss, touch, and sleep together. Remembering the day before in the bare attic room looking over Jared's floating house, Toby cleared his throat, struggling not to get hard. Jesus!

"I haven't had it cut in a while, Ellen," Toby contradicted the makeup artist as she patted his skin deftly. At first, it had been embarrassing, all this attention when he was wearing nothing but his hated cock sock, but now he was used to it. The people on set were sensitive and professional for the most part.

"I mean, uh, lower down." Ellen raised her brows, hazel eyes amused. She was about Toby's height, with cinnamon-tinted hair, one of his favorite people since she was always joking and he liked being the recipient of her curiosity and friendliness.

Abruptly Toby groaned. Shit, he'd forgotten about the hair cut down *there* Sahara Blue had given him. It was going to start growing back soon, but Jared had said he'd take care of Toby's hair removal from now on and that they'd both enjoy it. Toby could just imagine what that would be like, soap suds, slow, hot kisses, Jared touching him all over, the slide of the razor against his skin—

Too bad for some reason it hadn't happened yesterday! Instead, Jared had withdrawn, barely spoken a word to him before saying he needed some space.

Toby knew he was being a loser, but it had hurt when Jared asked him for that. If they were still just friends, he'd probably have taken it in stride, but the lover thing was giving him a whole new sensitivity.

"Toby, I didn't know you cared," Ellen teased now.

"Oh *man!*" Blushing furiously, Toby grabbed a towel and put it over his front parts. See what thinking of Jared and showers did to him?

"Is it for Anita?" Ellen asked. "The shaving thing, I mean." Now she blushed a little too.

"No."

Ellen raised a brow at Toby's automatic response.

"Um. Shit." Toby accepted a robe and belted it gratefully around his slim waist.

She waggled her brows and whispered, "Is it for Jared?"

Toby's eyes rounded. Oh shit! "How did you…?"

Ellen shrugged. "Just a feeling I've had for a long time about you two. You have such wonderful chemistry on screen that a girl can dream, right?"

"You find the idea of two guys…?" Toby shook his head, his face scarlet as Ellen chuckled. "Never mind, I don't think I want to know! And please keep it to yourself, okay?"

"You're at that stage when you don't want people to guess, right? When it's so new it feels too much to let on what's happening."

Toby gave her an uneasy glance.

"Oh, and the gay thing too. Toby…." Ellen chewed on her bottom lip. "The way you let Jared touch you, talk to you; it never seemed like just friends to me. It might sound corny, but it was like he was destined to be your lover."

"I didn't see it back then," Toby admitted. "I hope like hell it wasn't that obvious to Anita." Had it been? Geez, if so, it would explain a lot of her anger. He just hoped his stepfather didn't find out any time soon. Toby needed to get used to these new feelings, to being with another man for the first time. "Does everyone else…?"

"We've all seen you with Anita, but if you weren't dating her, I think people would have made some assumptions."

Toby sighed. "Yeah. It's just so new; I do need to keep it to myself. Besides." Now he chewed his lip, wanting to pump Ellen for information because he knew she'd done Jared's make up an hour before his own. Usually Jared hung around and waited for Toby, but not today for some reason. It was pricking at Toby, making him uneasy.

"Ummm?" Ellen lifted a brow.

Toby shook his head. "Never mind."

"He's in his trailer, I think," Ellen said, smiling.

"I don't want to push myself on him all the time, you know?" Toby said, feeling insecure, despite wanting to be with Jared before they had to make it a work thing.

"Push yourself? That man is deeply in love with you. Everyone knows," Ellen said. "Come on, your scenes? No one is *that* good an actor."

Toby picked up the velvet bag he'd brought especially today. He shook out its contents, showing it to Ellen shyly.

"Wow! That is *so* Jared. You really are in love with him, aren't you?"

JAI TOOK a deep breath as he entered Jared's trailer, finding his friend wearing a silk robe and lying in front of a small altar dedicated to Kwan Yin. Various eclectic items were arrayed around her sad, forgiving face: driftwood, bits of crystal, a theater ticket and a photograph of Toby and Jared, arms around each other, swigging beer and sporting goofy smiles and sunburned faces.

It wasn't hard to see the heart of his friend.

"Am I interrupting?" Jai asked softly. "Hey, I finally made it down to see the set since I had some business in the area."

Jared didn't respond and Jai blinked, realizing that his friend was asleep! It was unlike him to slip from meditation into sleep. Perhaps he'd been having trouble resting lately?

Frowning, Jai sat next to Jared, protective instincts triggered. In truth, he'd come down here to check on Jared because he was worried about him. Had his Toby hurt him?

ON SOME level, Jared knew he was dreaming, but went he caught Jai's familiar amber cologne, his dreaming mind sought escape and familiar comfort.

Jared turned around from where he knelt at the altar in his dressing room, blinking reddened eyes. He could see that Jai immediately guessed his sore eyes were not from the coiling incense at his altar. "Jared," he breathed, as if feeling regret. It seemed that they both had given themselves and stumbled. It made him wonder again if this pain was worth it. Right now he wished he'd never tried to be with Toby, never taken him to the special room, no matter how satisfying, how perfectly they seemed to fit.

Jai knelt beside his friend, cupping his cheek. "What is wrong, Jared?"

Jared's hands reached up and snagged him closer, like a drowning man, and next thing his mouth was pressed against Jared's. Jai tensed, as if knowing they needed to talk, as if knowing Jared was in a bad place.

"Jai, I need this—" Jared's tone was tormented to his own ears.

"But Toby—you love him. I know you do."

But I don't want to love him, Jared thought. It hurts to love Toby.

SAHARA BLUE was pacing, looking out at the water, still unable to get any rest and he was played out. He had a job as a bodyguard, no stretch for a man of his deadly talents, and soon it would be time to go to work. He worked for a company that provided personal security to celebrities and other people who needed special protection while in the San Diego area.

He had to be alert for work, so he'd probably pick up some energy cola on his drive to an office building where he'd be shadowing a Japanese businessman for a few hours, making sure he was safe.

But for right now.... He rubbed the back of his tense neck muscles, feeling swept by an undertow of his own making.

Lotus.

The name itself was something he found himself pondering, wondering at what it meant to the man who had chosen it. Did he mean it to symbolize finding harmony?

Sahara smirked as he wondered what the guy would make of meeting someone with his own unlikely name. Lotus was surely an online identity, but Sahara Blue was a real name, picked out by his seventies hippy Mom, probably while she was doing something recreational.

Finally, he gave into the temptation of months and returned to his laptop before he chickened out again. He dipped down to posts from the one at the top, since he was afraid his comment might be passed over. He didn't want anyone to see that, even if it was just some online thing.

He typed, *Are you as lonely as I am?*

Stared at the words, so bald. Jeez, he couldn't say *that,* could he? Way to show some finesse. Maybe he could think of something funny to say, even though he could never think of anything clever and so hated the pickup scene. He had to settle for guys who took him out on a test drive based on his looks, not on his ability to be articulate, and that always made him feel worse, somehow, like he was a big prick and some nice hair and muscles and not the teddy bear that Jared sometimes called him.

He parted his lips, thinking maybe if he worded it aloud he'd think of something—

But then his watch beeped.

Time was up. Time to go to work.

Heart pounding, he pressed enter.

GIFT for Jared clenched in one fist, Toby grazed his hand against Jared's closed trailer door, taking a deep breath. He could feel uneasy ground between himself and Jared, and unlike how it had been with Anita, Toby found that it was unacceptable. He didn't know what was happening, but he was willing to face it, to talk about it.

Because Jared was worth it.

You really are in love with him.

Yes, he was. And it was time to let Jared know, to make his stand. Maybe he knew nothing about how to be with another guy, maybe he was afraid, but it was time.

Toby grasped the knob into Jared's trailer.

Chapter 16

"*TOBY!*"

Toby flinched, knowing that voice anywhere. And he hated that his first instinctive response was to flinch.

He swallowed, turning to confront his stepfather, Mike Danvers, the last man he needed to see right now as he was going to his male lover to tell him that he—

Toby took a deep breath, bracing himself.

Mike strode over to confront him, hands on his hips, red hair tangled by the breeze off the ocean that was stirred up enough today to even make it to the permanent set for the soap, bringing the scent of fresh, bracing sea salt and reminding Toby of the sanctuary he'd found in Jared's floating home.

Toby met his stepfather's green eyes straight on, despite the sweat that broke out in his armpits and forehead. He hated confrontations and from the beginning, he and Mike had never seen eye to eye, always arguing.

"Anita told me you broke up with her," Mike said in flat disbelief, getting directly to the point. Or, to Toby, feeling like he was going straight for the jugular.

"Mike, can we talk about this some other time?" Toby asked. "I'm due on set soon."

Mike's gaze ran over Toby's robe, which shielded his almost-nudity. Toby flushed, knowing what Mike was thinking but he continued to hold Mike's gaze, not backing down.

"Going to shoot more gay porn, huh?"

Toby closed his eyes, noticing the gaffer and his assistant walking by. They no doubt caught Mike's words but they smiled at Toby sympathetically. However, Mike's visit and attitude would be all over set by the end of the day. Peachy.

"Yes, I am." *It's not just pretending with Jared anymore, Mike. And wouldn't you love to know that.* But this wasn't the time to reveal the truth. He couldn't avoid telling his stepfather sometime, but he could choose his ground.

"So who is the new girl?" Mike crossed his arms. "Do I know her? Are you going to bring her home so your Mom and I can meet her for dinner on Sunday?"

Just then, Jared's trailer door opened. Jared stepped out, looking sleepy and out of it, his robe falling off one shoulder. A man with a smoothly muscled body and a sensual face was close behind him, possessive hand wrapped around Jared's arm.

Toby wanted to growl. Was this the mysterious Jai at last? He wanted his goddamned hands off Toby's Jared!

"Toby," Jai greeted him in a soft voice. He flushed at Toby's direct stare. "Jared described you perfectly."

Jared was blinking at Toby, looking washed out and a little groggy.

"I, uh, was just coming to see you," Toby rasped.

"I was sleeping," Jared said, his face a closed door, not letting Toby in. Then Jared's jaw hardened when he noticed Mike Danvers, someone he'd met a few times.

"Mr. Danvers," he greeted Mike politely.

Mike grunted, but then pushed on his inquisition of Toby: "What's the name of the girl you're seeing now?"

Toby flushed under Jared's narrowed eyes. Oh shit.

"Why do you think I'm seeing someone?" he deflected.

"No guy would dump a fine girl like Anita to be on his own." Mike shook his head. "She and I both can't believe you aren't pursuing her right now, trying to win her back."

"Look, about that. I'd like to come by the house." It flashed through Toby's mind to wonder how Mike had found out so soon about his break up with Anita. And why did he think Toby had been the one to dump her?

"I knew it! I told your Mom you had to have met someone special!" Mike continued. "Not that Anita wasn't. I'm sorry about that gal. Always liked her and thought she might light some ambition in you."

Jared raised a cool eyebrow at Toby and Toby shut his eyes a moment. Already something was wrong between him and Jared, and the other two men being here was not giving them a moment to hash it out. Did he really have to go on set and play Jared's lover with this cloud hanging over them?

GWEN ANDERSON, the director's PA, bustled over, clipboard in hand. She smiled at both robed men as if oblivious to the tense atmosphere. "Time, Jared. Oh, Toby, we need you too."

"Perfect!" Toby took a deep breath, wishing he could just go back to his apartment, hole up with a beer, and bury his face against his knees.

Why had he ever thought it was a good idea to put himself in his best friend's hands? But was he still Toby's best friend, after this experiment in getting closer? Right now he seemed a stranger, unapproachable, guarded.

Toby looked at Jared, sensitized to a weird vibe between him and Jai. A vibe he'd been afraid he'd discover between them from the beginning, with him on the outside. "Good thing I trust you," he said with false lightness and a leaden gut as they followed Gwen. "Jai's... attractive."

"I trusted you, too, Toby," Jared muttered.

SAHARA BLUE jerked awake at the pounding. Shit! What the fuck?

He lurched up from the couch where he'd crashed, taking two steps and then opening the door, blinking at the bright sunshine that burned into his eyes, made all the brighter from reflecting off the mirror of surrounding water.

Toby shoved inside, red eyed, hands on his hips, steam practically coming out of the top of his head in silent cartoon frustration.

Great. Sahara was totally trashed from work and from thinking about the unattainable Lotus who had not responded—yet—to Sahara's comment on his blog. A pissy Toby was just what he needed. Why had he known that something was going to go wrong between Toby and Jared? Maybe because Jared cared too much, lacking the detachment that made him a superlative lover with other men.

And Toby was totally insecure, like a fawn in a new environment. As if to underline that point, he gave Sahara a look very like a lost deer and Sahara sighed, not happy to be proven right.

"What's wrong?" he asked, shoving his bed hair out of his eyes and crossing his arms.

"Why do you think something's wrong?" Toby demanded, pacing, his fists balled.

Sahara laughed. "I can't imagine. Are you pissed?"

"Yes!" Toby growled. Then he blinked. "Oh, you mean drunk. I had two beers."

"Forgive me for saying it, but I've noticed you don't hold them very well. How about some bad coffee?" Sahara raised an eyebrow and gestured toward his small kitchen.

TOBY sighed and followed Sahara into his galley kitchen, leaning against the cupboard and watching him. This place wasn't full of crystals and new age music and incense like a certain floating house a few yards away. Instead it was utilitarian, but in a way there was a familiar barrenness here. Toby looked around at the sparse mugs, the old coffee maker—not the kind you'd get for anyone but yourself, not the kind you'd have if you ever had anyone over for breakfast, say, as Jared did often.

Toby's mouth tightened at the thought.

Was Jared over at his place now, spending time with Jai?

"You don't get out much, do you?" he said, accepting the coffee from Sahara, whose brilliant blue gaze rose from resting on his hand as he wiped the counter in the wake of coffee making.

"Did Jared talk about me?"

"No," Toby growled, thinking he wouldn't be here if Jared had talked too much about Sahara. Apparently he was turning into a possessive man—nothing like the easygoing guy he'd always been over Anita.

"No, I don't get out much," Sahara agreed morosely. "How'd you guess?"

"Your place looks like my apartment. Kind of wallflower-guy, you know?"

Sahara sighed and leaned against his fridge, settling in companionably and Toby found himself trusting him more now. Perhaps because he'd let Sahara wield a razor around his sensitive parts. Turned out that was a great equalizer.

"Yeah. I'd like to see, uh, people."

"Other guys."

"One guy," Sahara admitted, eyes going to the closed door of his study.

"That online thing?" Toby asked. The guy was gorgeous, a walking wet dream and he was living like a shut-in. Huh.

"It's a safe outlet, I guess, but it's surprising how easily someone can hurt you, even when they are probably gazillion miles away."

"The dial tone or the busy signal?"

"The dial tone," Sahara admitted, lips lifting ruefully. "He hasn't bothered to answer my comment. Which maybe was pretty pathetic."

"Ouch. Well, he wouldn't do that if he could see you."

Sahara sighed and Toby took another sip of his coffee. It wasn't bad. Not all full bodied like Jared's with cinnamon or some shit in it, but it tasted homey. Like Toby's bad coffee.

"I'd rather he like me for my soul."

"Wow." Toby blinked.

"I know. Lame."

"I didn't know you were Bambi."

"Fuck you." But Sahara was smiling a little, and he looked a little less sad. "What's up with you and Jared?"

"Nothing."

"And that's the problem."

"It's just not going to work out. I mean, he's been acting all strange lately. He left work today without even really talking to me."

"Right, I guess that's why he's pacing his living room even now."

"Huh?" Toby blinked. "How do you know that?"

"My psychic powers, clearly. Okay." Sahara held up a hand. "His place is directly parallel to mine, so I can see it rocking up and down the way it does when he's restless. Usually in the past that's been over you."

"He and Jai—"

"Whoa. Jai? He's just Jared's friend."

"Yeah, his *friend*." Toby was feeling sulky, but he didn't give a shit. He didn't want another man to be closer to Jared than he was.

"That's all they are." Sahara's gaze was level.

"Come on, they're…." Toby put the coffee aside and raked a hand through his hair, pacing Sahara's living room. Fortunately, there wasn't much furniture to block his path.

"Friends with benefits."

"I guess that's common." Toby was despondent. He knew he was feeling sorry for himself. He just couldn't seem to help it. It hurt that Jared was shutting him out and he was searching for the reason behind it.

Sahara took another swallow of his coffee. "It's common for anyone single and lonely. Is this a problem with facing the fact you're gay? Jared worried about this, but I've thought...." Sahara shook his head. "Truth is, the way you looked at him sometimes, I figured where there's smoke...."

Toby looked away, taking in the view of the harbor, the gulls that flew low, sweeping the sea for signs of food.

Sahara walked over and took Toby's wrist gently, as if to capture his attention. "Wasn't there always something there between you two?"

Toby cleared his throat. "Yes. He was part of what I was searching for."

"Nice to meet you, Toby," Sahara said, putting out his hand, brows raised.

"It's okay to wish your life was easier?"

"Of course." Toby shook Sahara's hand. "That's a big step right there to getting what you want. Or who."

Toby's eyes pricked, and he swallowed thickly, but *this* was truly why he'd crashed Sahara's place, because he'd sensed that the other man could help him find his way back to Jared. Understand Jared.

"He pushed me away. It hurt, and I was feeling insecure. Then today he was all cozy with Jai."

Sahara Blue's eyebrows rose at Toby's bald statement. "He had to have a reason."

Toby nodded, feeling annoyance rise for the first time. *But why hadn't Jared talked to him?*

"Are you being honest with him about everything?" Sahara Blue asked mildly.

Toby caught his breath, sweat breaking out on his forehead. "But you said—!"

Sahara reached for his coffee again, waiting on Toby.

"You said he wouldn't film me or his bedroom while he was away. Not without telling me." Toby sat down heavily on Sahara's couch, remembering Jared's strange words, *I trusted you, Toby.*

"He wouldn't. That would be something he'd never do, not without your permission."

"But..." Toby covered his mouth with a cupped hand, feeling abruptly queasy. He had never meant for Jared to know about that slip with Anita, the bizarre post-break-up sex fueled by Toby's insecurities. He'd never, ever have chosen to hurt Jared that way. But what if he somehow had found out?

"Oh shit. Do I want to know?" Sahara rubbed the back of his neck, long sandy hair shifting over his neck like pale ropes. His vivid disco necklace caught Toby's eye, and he focused on that rather than Sahara's eyes, which he couldn't meet.

"I slept with Anita."

"Slept? Oh shit, you mean in *Jared's* house?"

Shit, that sounded so bad. That sounded like something no boyfriend in his right mind would ever forgive.

Toby couldn't speak. He was sweating now, shaky. He nodded.

Sahara Blue sat down next to him, reached out, tentative, and put an arm around him. "Toby...."

A sudden, hesitant knock on Sahara's door interrupted the moment.

"YOU came to him," Jared gritted, wearing a black wife-beater and jeans with engine grease on his chin. He had probably been doing something with his car before he'd returned to his home to pace. "You were pissed I was with Jai, but then you came here to Sahara's place."

Stunned, Toby stared at Jared. *Jealous.* Jared was jealous that he was here with Sahara!

"No." He listened to his instincts and went to him anyway, placing a hand on his arm. "No, there is no one else for me but you."

Jared gave a bitter laugh. "Except Anita." He took a deep breath and scrubbed his beard shadow, the sound rasping loud.

Jared knew! Knew about what had happened between Toby and Anita. Oh God, he'd guessed correctly the reason for his withdrawal.

"Come sit down," Toby invited, very gently. He had been in love with this man for a long time, but he'd been blind to seeing it. Now was it too late?

Jared took another deep breath, letting his head fall back a moment, his chest rising and falling rapidly. He paced, his posture stiff and not typically relaxed and open, signaling he was still feeling jealous, territorial. Fuck, they were a pair, Toby thought.

"SOMETHING for you," Sahara said softly, giving Jared a small glass of amber fluid after he sat on Sahara's couch. He drank it, his face blank, but then he blinked, looking up at his host.

"I'm sorry," Jared rasped. "I can't believe I—" He shook his head. "I know you'd never do something to hurt me."

"No, I wouldn't," Sahara agreed, solemn. "You suck, Jared."

Jared laughed and Sahara patted his shoulder. "I think I'll take a walk."

"You don't have to—" Toby protested.

"Yeah, I do." Sahara shrugged. "Better than sitting around here, imagining some guy who probably thinks I'm a loser." He snagged his coat and was out the door before either Jared or Toby could argue further.

Jared sighed. "Maybe it's a good thing he gave us some space."

"So you can break up with me?" Toby hated himself for asking, for sounding so needy and selfish. "Not that I'd blame you."

"I didn't do anything with Jai," Jared clarified. "I had a dream about him, I admit, and maybe you picked up on that vibe, but it was all about needing comfort. All about you, really, if you think about it."

"I wish I could say the same thing, that I'd been faithful, but the truth is Anita came over when you were away, and I was... I felt like I'd screwed things up with us. That you couldn't wait to get away from me." Toby swallowed, wishing he didn't have to share this with Jared and hurt him. Fuck! "She was familiar. I knew what to do to please her."

Jared was breathing deeply and his hands were clenched on his knees. "I understand," he gritted.

"But you're not okay with it."

"Would you be okay with it, if I did that with Jai?"

"*No.*" Toby couldn't hold himself back, he moved closer to Jared, the man he'd hurt, betrayed. "Jared, it makes no…difference, I know, but I didn't…" Toby blew out a breath. "I couldn't come with her."

"I'm glad," Jared growled. He shook his head. "I'm a bit primal about you and her. I guess I feel insecure too, but I watched you with her for years and she had everything I'd ever wanted."

Jared's arm pulled him close and Toby rested his face against Jared's neck, breathing his scent. "How did we get so lost?"

"I don't know. Maybe when I decided to run rather than stick my ground with you. I had the best of intentions."

"Me too," Toby admitted. "You're hot and confident and have a dozen men. I'm just a guy who cleans pools part time."

"I wish sometimes I wasn't your first," Jared confessed. "I'm terrified."

AFTER a long time sitting there on Sahara Blue's brown couch, staring at the sun on the water, Toby took a deep breath. "I think what we need is a fresh start."

"Toby—"

Toby put his hand up, firm now. He'd really been the one to rope Jared into this thing with him, never mind that Jared liked to tie *him* up. So now he had to convince Jared they could work this shit out. "I know I don't deserve a second chance."

"This can't work." Jared rubbed his eyebrow. "Can it?"

Toby laughed. "I don't know."

"It really hurt," Jared whispered.

"I know." Now Toby was solemn.

Jared swallowed. "You promise she's your ex now?"

"Jared—"

"Because it'll kill me if she takes you from me."

Toby rubbed Jared's back. "I didn't want to see you, to see myself, and as unfair as it is to her, she was maybe a part of that."

"And now?"

"And now I see you," Toby said.

Jared swallowed. "What next?"

"Next I'd like to show you my intentions are honorable." Humor lit Jared's gaze as Toby played with his fingers and stared up into his warm brown eyes. "I'd like to take you out on a real date, Jared Asche."

Chapter 17

"DID you get *any* sleep?" Sahara Blue asked around six sharp the next morning. He yawned, wearing a pair of silky sleep pants that were barely hanging on to the bare bones of his hips. He wasn't wearing a shirt for once, and he didn't see Toby's glance at his back as he opened the fridge.

Toby made himself look away before Sahara noticed the direction of his gaze.

He was sitting at Sahara's breakfast bar, which he had in place of a more traditional dining table—another sign of how isolated Sahara was. Anita had always insisted that dining tables were multi-purpose for entertaining and therefore not going out like many designers claimed. Not that Toby had cared, other than when she dumped him, she'd taken her battered farm table with her.

But who was he going to have over for dinner anyway?

He chewed his lip. Well, maybe one person.

Was candlelight done between two men? He needed a gay Dear Abby to fill him in. He gave Sahara a dazzling smile and the other man dipped one eyebrow, not looking impressed. "No."

"Hey, I didn't even ask you yet!" Toby reached for the hot egg and salad wrap he'd walked up to the wharf to buy that morning at one of the food stands. "But I bought you breakfast. Actually, it was the least I could do to thank you for letting me stay here, clear my head for a bit."

And avoid Mike and his mother and Anita's calls. He had the feeling they'd dropped by his place. But he needed to set that aside right now, his family's wanting to butt into his life. He needed to focus on this new, tentative olive branch between him and Jared.

Sahara took the wrap, pouring out orange juice for both of them and then starting up the coffee maker. He quirked his lips when he spotted the fine Seattle beans sitting on his counter that Toby had also deposited. "You saw Jared this morning."

Toby tried to stop the smile from dawning on his face.

"Geez, you two!" Sahara shook his head in mock disgust. "So it's okay?"

"It's us both being very careful. I only saw him for about two seconds since we were both grabbing breakfast. I wanted to kiss him on the dock, but I don't want to rush things and, I'm still dealing with accepting shit. It felt like I'd be pushing myself for him and not for me, you know? And I know Jared wouldn't want that." He was babbling, he knew, but he was bubbling like the perky coffee maker. "Plus, I think we both need to take it easy after...." Toby's voice drifted off, and he gave a one-sided shrug.

"Mmmm." Sahara finished with the machine and poured coffee for both he and Toby. "So what do you need from me?"

"You don't mind helping me out?" Toby reached out, brushed Sahara's arm. He had been a good guy throughout this.

"Toby, would you have come here if you thought I'd be the type who did?" Sahara blinked sleepy blue eyes, rubbing the bristle on his cheeks. He was actually pretty hot first thing in the morning with his sun-bleached blond hair mussed around his face.

And geez, wasn't he getting gayer by the moment? But hadn't he had these thoughts about guys for years, but shoved them aside as unacceptable? Taking the gay soap had been his big break for freedom. No wonder his stepfather had disapproved. He'd been right about Toby all along.

Shit, he wasn't going to think of his family now. One step at a time.

"No, I felt comfortable with you," Toby admitted. "In some ways, I feel like we have some stuff in common. Also, you're close to Jared."

"Well, Jared approved of you crashing here; I think he still needs to keep you safe." Sahara Blue rolled his eyes at this because Jared had stayed late the previous evening, even helping Toby make up the couch and then stroking his hair and whispering to him until he'd fallen asleep.

Remembering, Toby grinned. "I never knew what it would be like to be romanced. It's something you miss out on as the traditional masculine partner."

"I happen to think you are very masculine and traditional," Sahara teased. "But Jared, yeah, you're lucky, man." Sahara let out a sigh.

"Thank you, kind sir," Toby teased back, in high spirits. He'd totally fucked everything up with Jared. And yet, they still had a shot. It had had him grinning off and on for hours, even at his own reflection in the mirror when he shaved this morning.

"So what had you up so early today? Other than your rendezvous with Jared for better beans."

"I have been making a list of dating ideas for Jared and me. But, uh, this is new territory for me. Will you hear them out?" Toby lifted his pencil, chewing on the end and watching Sahara move into the living room and slouch in the hanging sixties chair which swung from the ceiling. Toby noticed he had a coral ring around one tanned ankle. He looked casual and California beach bum.

"I'll do what I can to help. Just, please, no *Titanic* reenactments at the bow of a boat, and we're good to go."

Toby's eyes widened. "People do that?"

Sahara rolled his eyes. "I had to fish someone out of the drink wearing a heavy dress who couldn't swim on bodyguard detail recently. Fell in when she and her fiancé did that 'flying thing' for wedding pictures."

Toby laughed and Sahara quirked a brow.

"No reenactments, promise."

"Okay. So what did you come up with?"

For an answer, Toby handed Sahara the list he'd made up, pacing as the other man read it.

"Whoa. Number three!" Sahara's eyes widened. "Shit!"

"Um." Toby crossed his arms. Then uncrossed them.

"You're going to do all this?" Sahara's eyes were a very bright blue. He looked happy for Toby and Jared.

"I thought eight to ten dates like this and he and I would be living together. It's what I've really wanted, right from the beginning if I was totally honest with myself, though I know he has doubts, legitimate ones. What do you think?"

Sahara laughed. "I think you're right."

JAI WAS meditating at Jared's altar in his bedroom. Seeing that, Jared left him alone and went into his great room, restless. He'd invited the other man to stay over on his couch the last night, but now he hoped Toby wouldn't misinterpret his kindness.

Seeing Toby this morning had been…. He'd looked in his blue eyes, touched his hair and felt the connection between them twisting in his gut.

Last night. Shit, they'd talked for hours! He'd stroked Toby's hair, the back of his hand, knelt beside him on Sahara's couch, leaned close for a gentle kiss.

He'd never had a night like that.

Yet even with this happiness bubbling up inside him, the shadowed part of himself wondered how was it that he could brush away so easily what had gone wrong? He was bruised.

Toby's issues with coming out; Anita, Mike Danvers, they were still there, waiting. And he knew that Toby had to deal with them, had to be honest.

"Jared," Jai's voice broke into Jared's brooding. "I think someone needs to meditate more than I do."

Jared nodded. "Yeah."

Jai gave him a hug. "I'm heading home this afternoon so you and Toby can be alone here again."

At that idea, Jared was smiling when he headed into his bedroom and knelt to light some incense.

"I THINK you should lead off with number seven," Sahara Blue said, electric razor buzzing over his jaw. He opened his closet as Toby slouched in the doorway of his bedroom.

"Whoa," Toby said, taking in all the expensive black suits and casual wear. He'd never seen Sahara in anything but beach bum wear.

"Bodyguard stuff," Sahara said. "I have to dress up for formal occasions and blend in. The company gives me a stipend for it."

"Number seven. I'll have to call and hope I can arrange something with the society responsible for the garden," Toby said, already chewing his lip, musing.

"I bet that place is amazing at night, with the lanterns lit," Sahara hinted.

Toby's eyes widened, picturing it. "I want to do it tonight!"

"Well, then, you better—"

But Toby was already on his BlackBerry, pacing, ignited. He reached the garden society president with his first try.

Jared. Tonight was for Jared.

JARED wiped some fresh engine grease from his forehead and sat up, tank top sticking to his chest. He had just finished doing a little work under his DeSoto, which constantly needed maintenance, but fortunately, he found it relaxing to work on the car. He was not unaware of Toby's gaze studying him thoroughly. He smiled, feeling a little shy, despite the stuff they'd done together. But now it felt all new, their fresh start.

"Hey," he said.

Toby handed him an iced tea and he gratefully drank some, resting the cool glass against his forehead.

"Hey back," Toby said. "Listen. I have it all arranged."

Jared raised his brows. "Ummm?"

"It's sexy when you say things like 'ummm', do you know that?" Toby said. "Or maybe I'm just totally crazy."

Jared grinned.

"Shit!" Toby laughed. "I'm out of control with you lately."

"I like you out of control," Jared drawled.

"Yeah, I know." Happiness and anticipation in Toby's eyes, but not the anxiety anymore that had been there when they'd first started exploring things sexually. Jared wondered if maybe it had been a good thing, the rough patch. It had shown them what they risked losing, and it had given Toby more time to adjust to being with another man.

"So what do you have arranged?"

"Our first date of ten I drew up this morning," Toby said, stroking the fins of Jared's car. The movement seemed suggestive, making Jared think of Toby stroking his body, his cock. Geez, cheesy. But he couldn't help that Toby brought out the buried lust monster inside him.

"Ten dates?" Jared blinked. "You're taking this very seriously."

Toby sobered. "Yeah. I know it's early for us, but I think maybe you're going to be the one, you know?" He cleared his throat. "I mean, I've been moving in your direction for months, years."

"Toby, I've been in love with you more than two years," Jared said. "But we have stuff."

"No, you mean, *I* have stuff." Toby swallowed. "I'm working on it. Let's take this first step."

"What if I want to kiss you in the parking lot of this place we're going?" Jared pushed, a little skeptical. He still remembered Toby pulling away from his cuddling on the wharf. He understood it, but they couldn't have a relationship if Toby was in hiding, ashamed of being with Jared. Coming out was different for everyone, but it would be acid washing over everything they tried to build together if Toby continued to turn away.

"Come here," Toby said, very softly. His eyes gleamed, but his lips parted, showing some trepidation.

Jared took a moment to give him a comprehensive look and then climbed to his feet, moving very slowly.

They were standing out in the open, in the parking lot for the moored boats and floating homes. Anyone could see them.

He and Toby stared at each other, the moment drawn out, and then Toby curled a hand into Jared's dark hair and Jared closed his eyes, making a rough sound.

Toby.

Slowly, Toby moved closer, until he was pressed against Jared. When Jared opened his eyes, he met uncertainty and determination and fire in Toby's gaze.

And then Toby's mouth sealed against his own and Jared grabbed Toby's ass and pulled him higher and they were kissing roughly.

Stroking Toby's tongue with his own, giving himself, enthusiastic, so they pulled away and Jared cursed. His boner was rubbing against Toby's body, unmistakable. "I'm going to need to put that inside you. Soon," Jared warned, huffing.

Toby didn't back off, but lifted his leg to curl around Jared's, a sign of surrender, desire for penetration.

Forgetting they were outdoors, Jared reached down and cupped Toby's swollen cock through his jeans, squeezing appreciatively.

"Jared!" Toby groaned.

"*Toby! What the fuck!*" The shocked and familiar female voice was a wakeup call, like burning whiskey thrown in the eyes.

Jared's arms went limp as Toby fell back, startled, staring at Anita, who was dressed in her work clothes, standing next to her open car door. She'd obviously driven down here to see her ex and gotten a hell of an eyeful.

"So you're pawing each other in public now? Very classy." Anita slammed the door of her Buick closed, mouth tight.

"I—" Toby shoved his hair back with a shaking hand.

Jared turned to confront Anita. It was time she knew they were a couple now. He put an arm around Toby's shoulders, though he still worried his new lover would be pulled away by everything Anita had to represent; safety and familiarity. And she was hot too.

"What do you want?" he asked her bluntly.

Anita's eyes widened and her blond hair swung in its ponytail as she confronted Jared as well as Toby. "I just spent about an hour calming down Mike Danvers."

Jared raised a brow, feeling Toby's tension as Anita's words shot home. "What business is it of yours?" he asked.

Anita glared at him. "Toby's my business."

"No, he is not," Jared said mildly. But then, heart pounding, he looked to Toby, let his arm fall away. Would Toby step back to sure ground? Jared couldn't promise him coming out would be easy or that their relationship would even work out.

Toby swallowed, locking eyes with Jared before turning to Anita again. "I'm not your business," he agreed, reaching for Jared's hand.

Chapter 18

NERVOUS, Toby watched from the back seat as the driver pulled in next to the long gate, ceramic round blue caps topping the elegant wood and stone, and beyond, the tall green trees swaying in the dusk breeze off the ocean. Jared was quiet beside him, but he was looking around, tracking familiar landmarks as they neared the garden entrance.

His lips parted as his new partner looked at him. He so wanted this date, their first real one, to go well.

They were holding hands, which made him think of the unpleasant scene with Anita until he pushed it aside.

Toby wasn't going to think about that now, or how after she'd left, he and Jared had gone to his floating house and Jared had sat on his couch and rubbed his lower back in gentle circles. Not trying to talk or tell Toby how to feel, since his gut was twisted and Toby had broken out in a cold sweat, his heart galloping.

He'd come out and he knew there was no going back. He knew that soon he'd have to face his family, that people at work would know, that they would look at him differently.

He was scared.

Jared's touch felt like the only thing in the world, grounding him, telling him that he'd be okay, that he'd adjust.

Toby's head had fallen forward and the phrase *this too will pass* had gone through his mind in response to Jared's silent support. He knew intellectually things would work out, but right now he wasn't sure how it was even possible. He had to fight off being swamped by pessimism, wondering if his family would cut him out of their lives.

After a while, Jared climbed to his feet and made green tea and lit some of his favorite Japanese *Autumn Leaves* incense, and they'd both holed up on the Kelim floor pillows by the floor to ceiling windows that looked out at the bay.

The waves crashed out at sea, over and over, the sun lighting each one, seeming to signal that life went on, that things would work out. And Toby went back to the night this all started, when he'd been sipping beer during his birthday party. He'd come a long way. He wouldn't have been strong enough to cut his ties with Anita back then.

He held the celadon tea bowl Jared had given him with chilled hands, but the steam had eventually warmed him, rising up like inevitable hope.

At last, he leaned his head against Jared's neck, feeling the rasp of Jared's dark early whiskers, glimpsing concerned warm brown eyes, relaxing slowly as Jared's fingers stroked up and down his back.

THE double wooden gate stood open, iron rings against light colored bamboo, and beyond the graveled path was lit by white lanterns, pale as cherry blossoms in the falling light.

Jared paused, dressed up in a charcoal blazer made of velvet and a black turtleneck and pants, silk and cotton for the warm climate. His dark hair was combed high off his forehead in silken swirls and he was freshly shaven, smelling of sandalwood and wearing a gold embossed chunky ring on his index finger.

Toby's gut twisted more pleasantly, taking in this man. *His man.*

Toby had dressed up for the occasion as well, wearing a dark wine cotton tee shirt and black jacket and pants. Sahara Blue had lent him some patchouli cologne he said Jared particularly liked. Since Jared had bent close to him as soon as they'd been alone in their chauffeured car and sniffed Toby's neck, his breath puffing against Toby's skin and sensitizing him, so he shivered at the touch of lips barely grazing flesh, he thought it was a damn good tip.

Toby had paid by credit card ahead of time for the special car and driver, so they left both behind them.

The attendant to the garden bowed as they passed him, and then after he and Jared broached the entrance, the man closed the door behind them, knotting it with rope.

Jared walked forward, tall under a maple tree with lacy leaves shifting softly in the twilight. The artificial lake beyond the high path reflected white lanterns that dotted the Japanese stroll garden, lit for this special occasion.

"They usually do this for weddings or anniversaries," Toby outlined, knowing that with Jared's interest in Eastern culture he had to have visited this garden a dozen times before. But never like this, at dusk, with white lanterns the shape of a full moon hanging from tree branches and white foil lanterns up-lighting large moss-covered boulders on their undulating path.

"Toby!" Jared breathed, putting his hands in his pockets as he walked forward a little way, his eyes wide with awe.

Toby's lips lifted. It had been a tough day, and this was like a cure-all for his bruised psyche, seeing the amazement on Jared's face. He realized that for a large part of their relationship, Jared had been the tour guide, taking him to new places.

But now Toby had taken Jared somewhere he'd never been, gifted him with a fresh adventure.

Jared reached for his hand and Toby took it, fingers clasping warmly as the gravel crunched beneath their feet, the only sound in the garden save for the soft movements of settling birds.

The air was warm, like a caress, stirring their hair as they walked past the towering grandfather lantern, festooned with a roof like curled scrolls, capped by a round top and snarling dragons; the empty cavity just above their heads lit by a little nest of spilling white lights and glittering with coins left by the garden visitors.

THEY walked counter clockwise through the garden, carefully navigating the large stones that bridged a running brook lit by a stone lantern halfway down its expanse. Even then, balancing in dress shoes, Jared didn't let go of Toby's hand.

When they reached the other bank, Toby felt as if this Japanese garden represented the journey he was taking with Jared. The landscape offering different obstacles as they moved forward. As he looked into Jared's solemn eyes, he thought he read similar sentiments.

They crossed the rainbow bridge, the appreciation and silence held between them broken by the sudden splash of a Koi fish leaping from the water below toward a night flying insect.

The tea house was waiting, twin guardian lanterns at each entrance lit, the shoji screen open pointedly at one end, welcoming them, looking over at the night garden and a rock fountain that burbled in a whispering grove of black bamboo.

Because both men had visited the garden before, they knew to go around to the side door where they could remove their shoes and socks, putting on sandals offered by the man who had let them into the garden. He had waited here to attend them, and Toby had the feeling the elderly man would have waited serenely for several hours, as if it made no difference how long it took them to make their journey through the garden.

The man bowed again and gestured to the small teahouse portion of the building. Sandals shushing over tatami mats, Jared and Toby entered the space and knelt with their backs to the outdoors, where the man bade them to sit with a welcoming smile.

"I can't believe you did all this!" Jared said, still wide-eyed with wonder. He looked like he was lost in a new world, in his perfect world, and right then Toby resolved that if they could make it work somehow between them, they'd take a trip together to Japan.

Toby's lips quirked as he watched the Asian man kneel in front of an old fashioned burner with formal tea supplies and also some elaborate black and cedar Bento boxes.

It took some time, watching as the man was lost in his ritual of preparation, but finally he offered one box to Jared, who sat at the place

Mastering Toby

137

of the first guest, closest to the attendant. He bowed and Jared bowed in response, opening his chopsticks and touching the display of his food gingerly. It was an amazing picture, seafood making up the pattern of a wave rising, foamy, and a tall mountain in the distance. Rice had been tinted three different soft colors with vegetable dyes: salmon, aqua and saffron, telling the story of a sun setting at sea. To the side in compartments were kabobs of meat, an egg chopped to resemble an open fan and various other delicacies.

Jared looked at Toby. "I'm almost afraid to eat it. You're spoiling me, boy," he drawled, the intimacy of the word *boy* a reminder of the sexual games they liked to play.

Toby shook his head, shifting a little as his cock responded to Jared's tone. "You waited for me for a long time. I want to show you that I appreciate it and it was worth it. I'm hoping things will get easier for us both from here on out."

The Asian gentleman finished tweaking Toby's bento box, which was a different shade of reddish colored wood from Jared's box, and bowed after offering it. Toby bowed back before picking up his chopsticks. Their servant for the evening discreetly left them alone to enjoy their meal, shutting the glowing yellow shoji door behind him.

Toby's food was arranged to resemble the flotsam washed up on a beach, even featuring some food which resembled sea shells. He tried one of the rice rolls, which were the soft green-gray of seaweed, closing his eyes as he enjoyed the piquant taste.

They had been offered simple containers of water to drink with their meals, so they sipped, still not speaking very much, as if this was the calm after the storm earlier in the day.

Toby's muscles still ached from being strung tight, but the tension seemed now to only emphasize this peaceful experience he was sharing with his new partner.

After they finished eating, their attendant returned with water to rinse their hands and they watched as he prepared macha tea, foamy and green. Jared fed Toby a sweet biscuit with a ginkgo pattern embossed on the pastry.

Tea bowls in hand, they turned at last to face the darkened garden, each leaning against one side of the tea house wall as they sipped and breathed in the night air.

"I bought you something," Toby said, having waited a while for this moment.

"Toby!" Jared laughed, clearly overwhelmed. "Baby, this is beyond anything I ever pictured. Just having you kiss me, let me make love to you. That's all I ever dreamed of, corny as it sounds."

"Well, I had Sahara Blue's help on this one," Toby continued, glad that his date seemed to be a hit. He wanted to push aside the dark shadows, his mistake with Anita, the looming thundercloud of a confrontation with his family. He wanted to create an oasis for the two of them that might bloom into a new life.

Toby pulled out the little blue velvet bag with its smooth lumpy contents and handed it to Jared, who paused to put down his black chunky hand-thrown tea bowl before shaking out the contents in one large palm.

Stones glittered, catching the lantern light, and Jared's eyes widened.

"The pendant is made of that stone you wanted me to have close to me that first time you went away, Laramir. I chose it myself from a rock shop with Sahara and they drilled it for us there. And the flat pebbles are blue crazy lace agate. I just thought... that vivid color against your olive skin...." Now Toby's voice tightened, as he had a sensual picture pop in his head of Jared wearing nothing but the necklace, perhaps climbing out of the water from a midnight swim off his floating house, hair slick off his forehead, his pubic hair a dark frame for the heavy sex that Toby would take in his mouth, making Jared cry out and cradle his head as Toby sucked him on his knees.

Color rose in Toby's cheeks at the erotic picture. Man, his visions of he and Jared were getting more and more intense. He cleared his throat and continued his explanation of the design of his offering. "The cut stones are yellow opal. Thought they'd go well with your eyes."

Jared unclasped the pendant and Toby lifted up so he could put it around his boyfriend's neck. He smoothed a hand over it, holding

Jared's gaze. "I want to see you wearing nothing but this," he admitted in a whisper.

Blue eyes caught by brown ones, Toby leaned closer and they kissed.

Jared groaned and lifted him immediately onto his lap, Toby's spread legs encompassing his body. Toby rubbed himself against the larger man, catlike.

"Boy, I can't keep myself from having you," Jared husked, pressing stinging little kisses against Toby's neck, his hand fisted possessively in Toby's hair. "I want to fill you, want to see my cock moving in and out of your ass."

For an answer, Toby reached down and cupped Jared's erection, holding Jared's gaze as he petted.

"Is this mine, Jared?" he asked, exploring Jared as his breathing grew more ragged and perspiration broke out visibly on his face.

"When you tease me like this, I want to share a bath with you in a big tub and maybe paddle your ass red before I bend you over the tub and fuck you," Jared growled.

Now Toby was panting, his body pulsing, his nipples, cock, all hard for Jared. He lifted his legs, wrapping them in a slutty fashion around Jared's waist.

"Toby, we have to hold off," Jared rasped.

Toby groaned agreement. They'd dressed up, and they were not alone, so they probably shouldn't. Somehow they had to wait, despite his desire to free Jared's clothing and impale himself on his hard prick.

"I've been using that kit you recommended," Toby said, unable to keep from nipping Jared's ear as the other man's big palms were full of his ass, pulling him closer. "The one to make it more comfortable for me to have you inside me."

"I'm not sure how comfortable it will be the first time. As soon as we get back to my place, I want you on the floor, your pants off, your ass high. I need to mount you," Jared outlined baldly. "If I can manage, I'll pull out and come on your ass. I want to see that, my come on you."

"Jared," Toby moaned.

Jared took Toby's hand in his and yanked him from the lighted tea house. The elderly man had disappeared discreetly, and they were alone in the dark garden.

Next thing Toby knew they were deep in the trees and Jared leaned against one suggestively, lifting his hands high, upraised palms above his head.

Toby fell to his knees, the motion seeming inevitable now, completely natural. His hands shook as he unhooked Jared's belt and opened his pants, tugging down silk boxers and nuzzling the hard prick he revealed.

His own cock throbbed, aching for touch, but Toby's master hadn't given him permission to work himself so he opened his mouth and took Jared inside him, losing himself in focusing on tasting him, pleasing him.

Above him, Jared maintained his pose, completely in control. His eyes gleamed satisfaction, his lips parted as Toby pleasured him. "My little cocksucker," he praised.

Chapter 19

SAHARA BLUE leaned forward, lips parted as he read Lotus's latest fantasy on his blog. His fingers were digging into his knees, sweat was breaking out on his forehead and the back of his neck, and his heart was pounding.

In a futuristic environment, I am handcuffed, naked, my arms behind my back as I am escorted into a cop shop. I am a natural submissive and I've been in hiding, living in the wild, but now I've been captured and I will be processed and given an owner.

I sit on a long bench, seeing the shadows of tall, busy men pass me, aware that I catch their eyes as they go about their business, examining my cock, which is hard.

After waiting a long time, almost all day by my reckoning, a towering man strides over. In my fantasy, he is of a slightly different breed of human, a large barbarian with a silken pelt of short fur covering his body so he is soft to the touch. He is also naked, save for a loin cloth.

He puts a collar around my neck and snaps a leash to it. One tug, and I get up from the bench and kneel at his feet. I wait as he fills out some kind of computer pad, taking ownership of me, and then a tag is snapped to my collar, bearing his name.

I am his.

He takes me back to his den, a luxurious cavern with rugs made of fur and handmade items, like chiseled wooden bowls and bright woven cloth—very pleasing to me since I'm so tactile. He doesn't speak to me or acknowledge me in any way, but points to a floor pillow near his bed...

"Shit, Lotus," Sahara grumbled. "How am I supposed to sleep now?" It was Lotus's weekly bedtime story hour, when he shared a fantasy scenario of himself in some exotic environment. Often Sahara found himself drawn into his world, like a diver suddenly yanked under water.

He was certainly drowning in Lotus; he was obsessed with him.

And depressed that so far he had not answered the slender and needy comment Sahara had left him.

Well, what do you expect? You sounded like a loser. He must have guys writing him all the time, propositioning him. Just because you printed up those grainy photos you think are of him, had them enhanced so you could study them. This is no more real than a celebrity crush.

Sahara got up from his chair, the floorboards creaking under his bare feet, his jeans unbuttoned but zipped as he went to the floor-to-ceiling window and looked out at the nightscape, needing the serenity of the view to calm his chaotic thoughts.

He closed his eyes and pressed his cheek against the wind-and-sea-cooled glass before opening them again to take in the view. His windows needed to be cleaned of salt residue soon. He'd get in his wetsuit and maybe do it tomorrow morning—

He frowned, his attention caught by a light on over at Jared's place. It was odd, bouncing over the walls like a yellow ball. No other lights showed in his friend's floating home.

But then, Sahara knew that couldn't be Jared. Jared was still out on his first special date with Toby.

"JARED."

Jared frowned at Sahara Blue calling to him at the gated entrance to the ramp down to the wharf. He was walking back from the hired car with Toby, his arm around the slighter man as he nuzzled his hair. He was feeling expansive, all his appetites appeased, although he knew his innocent was still simmering and needing release. But that pleased him, too, that Toby would wait until he was permitted by Jared to let himself go. He was counting on that to give them a memorable first time.

What an amazing date they'd had! He'd never…. He swallowed thickly, recognizing that Toby had wanted to give him the Disney moments. Wanted to romance him.

Could Toby really love him?

Now he blinked at what he saw in Sahara Blue's strained face as the other man watched Jared and Toby approach.

It took a moment to switch gears from the wonderful evening as he tensed. "What's wrong? Are you okay? Is it Jai?"

Sahara swallowed, opening his mouth to speak but shook his head before his tangled beach bum hair hid his expression.

His attitude grabbed Jared by the throat, making his heart pound. Toby pulled away from him and went to Sahara, taking his arm, asking with his eyes what was wrong.

Sahara looked up again, his eyes brimming with tears, chewing his lip.

Then he looked at Jared.

Bad, it was bad.

"I NEED to do this alone," Jared whispered, dropping Toby's hand as they reached his seventies bungalow-style floating home.

Toby opened his mouth to argue, instinctively disagreeing, but Sahara squeezed his arm, shaking his head silently. In an undertone, he said, "Let him, Toby. He needs to…." But Sahara's voice again dried up, as if he couldn't think of the words.

Toby's dress shoes, still immaculate from his and Jared's perfect first date, crunched on the shattered glass of the beautiful heron etched door as its ruin sparkled in shards on the teak flooring.

"I told him that door was asking for a burglar to break in," Sahara noted sadly. "But Jared always said 'who would do that?' His stuff wasn't worth money, man. It was how he put it together."

Toby knelt down and picked up the heron's wing, remembering how many times he'd looked at Jared through that glass, Jared beckoning him inside with a nod of his head and a smile touching his lips.

He knew that Jared had commissioned it from a local Native American artist and he'd had her over for breakfast and dinner a few times so she'd have a sense of the environment, the light on the water.

The door was a work of art and could never be recreated.

Aching, Toby found all the bits of glass with the focal pattern, not sure why, but it seemed something constructive to do.

He didn't know he was crying silently until Sahara Blue pulled him into his arms and he muffled a sob against his shoulder, hand fisted in his T-shirt.

"I'm all right, I'm all right," he said a moment later, dashing moisture from his eyes. He hadn't even seen the worst of it, just a broken door hanging open.

And right now Jared was in there, alone.

An officer caught Toby's eye, his blue shoes crunching over the same broken glass that Toby's had as he stepped off the pier and onto Jared's entranceway. "I'm Officer Martinez. You are a friend of the victim?" he asked.

Taking a deep breath, Toby nodded. "I'm Toby Rafferty, a co-star of Jared's on *Mission Bay.*"

"Oh, yeah, I've watched it. You guys have a lot of chemistry. So you're a good friend, huh?" Martinez was scrawling notes down, and Toby had the sense he knew exactly what kind of friend, but was okay with it. He felt relieved that at least the investigating officer wasn't a homophobe. Jared didn't need that right now.

"Yes," he rasped. He looked through the open door and could see the saffron and ruby dyed pillows, the Kelim he often wrapped himself in. They were torn up, debris scattered on the hardwood floor.

And then he saw it.

Jared's favorite mandolin.

"*Oh no.*" Toby cupped his mouth as fresh tears pricked his eyes. Jared hadn't played for a while, not since this thing had started between them, but it wasn't uncommon for him; he would have dry spells as a musician sometimes before his muse would pick him up like an eagle flying, and he'd soar for a while, writing music, performing in small clubs. Toby had gone to see him several times, sipping a beer and staring up at Jared on stage.

The handmade instrument, created by someone in Wales especially for Jared, was broken in half over his couch, the strings curled like shriveled fall leaves.

"Oh no," he repeated.

"I'm sorry, I know this is hard," Martinez sympathized quietly, grabbing Toby's attention again.

Toby nodded.

"This house was an easy mark, unfortunately. No door brace or security system, not even surveillance cameras or stickers on the windows to dissuade home invasion," the cop continued, looking over the wreckage with experienced eyes.

Sahara nodded. "I suggested he use dummy cameras. Just as effective."

"Yeah, good suggestion from the former Navy SEAL," Martinez continued, nodding respectfully to Sahara Blue. "Unfortunately, I don't think that there is going to be much coming from insurance." Martinez sighed.

Toby's jaw hardened. He took a deep breath and headed for the door, shards sticking to his shoes.

"Toby."

This time he chose to ignore Sahara Blue's warning. Jared had had enough time seeing this, alone.

INSIDE the great room seemed another place from the home Toby had last visited, like one of those dystopian future worlds where civilization has failed and everything lies in ruins. That was the only way that Toby could make sense of why every single one of the windows looking out to sea were shattered, why the floor pillows had been torn open with a kitchen knife, why all of Jared's mandolins, four of them that had once hung proudly like works of art on the cedar wall, were scattered like broken carcasses on the floor.

And there was more. The kitchen cupboards stood open, revealing all Jared's colorful majolica pottery in pieces. The microwave was on the floor, the fridge was open, the food strewn out and stomped on.

Toby took another unsteady breath.

This wasn't a simple home invasion.

This was hate.

He passed the bathroom, feeling like he was walking through a nightmare. Jared's nightmare. There was an ache under his breastbone and his eyes stung again as he stepped over Jared's razor next to ripped up Egyptian cotton towels in the jewel colors that Jared preferred; in the bathroom he also glimpsed the white framed vintage mirror, crazed from a blow.

He found Jared at last in his bedroom.

He was kneeling in front of his altar, a familiar pose, but where Kwan Yin had once smiled sadly, the statue was headless, broken like the bedroom window that looked out at the lights dotting the harbor in blurry dabbles.

Cold night air drifted in.

Jared's bamboo dresser was open. His clothing was torn, his collection of stones were missing—thrown out the window into the ocean?—the small wireless speakers were smashed, and his toy drawer, the one Toby had found, the blown glass dildos, the silk scarves in bright, life-affirming colors were shattered, ripped, looking like broken ornaments.

Toby made a soft noise. That drawer had been something he'd looked forward to exploring with Jared.

Jared turned his head and looked into Toby's eyes. He was crying.

Toby strode to him, and regardless of the mess, knelt behind him, wrapping his arms around him firmly.

Jared was shivering.

Toby waited and finally Jared said huskily, "Well, I have one set of good clothes that didn't get tossed overboard or ripped in half." It was a joke. A sad one.

Toby pressed his face against the back of Jared's neck, hot tears pressed against chilly skin. "Jared, I'm so sorry."

Jared's body hiccupped one harsh sob; his hand went up, covering his mouth, obviously trying to ride out the pain.

"Jared." Toby kissed his ear and then tongued it instinctively.

And Jared turned around in Toby's arms, his forehead nuzzling Toby's and then his lips caught Toby's in a hard kiss, his hand fisted in Toby's hair. He pulled away at last, panting.

"Lock the door!" he commanded softly.

"But—" Toby thought of the cop outside, of Sahara Blue, but then without another word he got up and shut it with a *snick*.

IT WASN'T a first time Toby would have ever imagined with his Jared.

Jared did not say a prayer first to Kwan Yin, though his fingers touched her headless body, grazing the lotus flower she held poised in her fingers. There was no lit incense, no candle light or any light except the soft oily sheen of lights off the water.

The room was cold, the puffing wind coming in through jagged gaps in Jared's window.

But there was Jared. Damp cheeks and a hand cupped around Toby's neck as they kissed, drinking from each other, both of them trembling, the moment, the emotion too strong to refine into meaning.

There was no meaning.

Everything was broken around them. All they had was each other.

Jared helped him pull down his pants, his black thong, and then threw a blanket over the debris. He croaked hoarsely, "Hands and knees, Toby."

Toby looked over his shoulder, seeing Jared open his pants and roll a condom on himself with shaking fingers.

He was still crying.

He spurted out too much lube on one hand and it was cold, making Toby jump a little on contact but he took a deep breath and forced himself to relax as fingers pushed inside, preparing him.

In the reflection of the mirror fallen to the floor at a crazy angle, he watched it happen in glimpses, though he shut his eyes when Jared mounted him and thrust inside without preamble.

"*Uh!*" Jared felt too big and it wasn't exactly comfortable, but more tears squeezed from his tightly closed lids as Toby willingly accommodated his lover.

Jared's hand ringed the back of his neck, pressing his head against a torn pillow from the bed while he thrust inside Toby's raised ass, grunting, his eyes flat hammered gold in the mirror, animalistic.

Toby felt Jared's hard prick brush against something that felt electrifying, making his own penis, which had softened at Jared's sudden entry, stiffen a little.

He breathed, watching Jared fuck him in the shadowed mirror, his hips recoiling and then pushing forward, smooth, graceful. Watched himself taking it, his arching back, holding steady for Jared's thrusts even as he experienced the alien feel of the heavy club inside him.

He thought there was a knock on the door, but neither of them answered, panting now, wide eyed as they both watched their moving bodies.

His thoughts were scattered like the broken glass. Pieces.

Jared was fucking him. He was getting fucked.

"Oh Toby. Oh!" Jared sped up, his body hammering into Toby now, his eyes fixed, blank. And then he grimaced, spurting, gripping Toby hard.

After, Jared pulled away, sitting with his clothing still open and his body sticky with cooling sweat. He stared out the window.

Toby winced as he shifted closer. His ass hurt.

He wrapped his arms around Jared again.

"Maybe I should just leave it," Jared said, voice aching with grief. "Just let it go. Toby, there's nothing left of me here."

Chapter 20

"IS HE still asleep?" Sahara Blue asked morosely as Toby tiptoed out of Sahara's bedroom and closed the door softly behind him.

Toby nodded, swallowing hard. His throat tightened as he thought of the difficult night, of holding onto Jared, of Jared not speaking, just staring numbly out the window toward his darkened home.

"Thanks for letting us have your bedroom," Toby said. "We could have gone to a hotel."

Sahara shook his head immediately, clearly not liking that idea. "He's shocky right now. He needs something familiar to hold onto, and right now that's you and me."

"Yeah," Toby croaked, tears welling. Shit, he had to stop this, but it hurt so much, watching Jared hurt. "We're about all he's got left."

Sahara gripped his shoulder, squeezing it firmly. "Then I'd say he's a pretty lucky man."

Toby gave a jerky nod. "Thank you," he said in a soft undertone, flushing a little.

"No problem." Sahara took a sip of his own coffee and then poured a mug for Toby. "So the stuff I gave you knocked him out?"

"Yes." Toby sipped his own coffee. "He was… I was glad when he fell asleep."

"It's easier than him hurting."

There was a knock on the door, and Toby scrubbed his bloodshot eyes, watching as Sahara went to answer it. He already knew who it would be, since he'd summoned him the night before when Jared had finally fallen asleep.

Jai walked in, delicate, smelling of warm amber cologne, brown eyes full of pain and concern. Without hesitation, he went to Toby and pulled him into his arms.

Toby was shocked at first, considering how he'd been so jealous of this man, but he felt himself gradually relaxing as he recognized instinctively the hug was genuine, the desire to comfort sincere.

"Jai, I'm glad you're here," Toby croaked. He cleared his throat, dashing his eyes again. Shit.

"Someone wanted to smash him, smash you both. Where else would I be?" Jai asked simply. He took the green tea that Sahara offered him in place of coffee.

"It wasn't a homophobic crime," Sahara said, eyes on Jared's floating home which usually this time of morning would typically offer a view of Jared making breakfast through his kitchen window, maybe a CD of flute music lightly dancing over the water to Sahara's open windows. "Not obviously, anyway. It seemed way more… personal."

"It was hate," Toby said flatly, taking a deep breath, remembering all the broken mirrors, almost like someone had struck them with a fist. "Someone hates him, like Jai said, wanted to smash him."

"Yes, and why now? What could Jared have done *now*?" Sahara's vivid eyes were sad as they flicked over Toby's tight face. "Something set someone off. Maybe it's not Jared someone hates."

Toby took a deep breath. "Shit. I hoped it was just me, thinking it; that it was about *me*. Someone angry that Jared and I…. That we love each other."

Jai rubbed Toby's shoulder, eyes lit with determination and care. "Then this person has failed, my friend; he or she only brought you closer."

Remembering their first time, feeling how his body was still sore, Toby nodded. He took another deep gulp of coffee, hoping it would give him strength.

He had a lot to do today.

"JAI, I need your recommendations on places that sell stones, Buddhas, incense, new age stuff. And we need to find him a new statue of Kwan Yin. She has to be very special."

Jai nodded. "I know a few places locally, though not one central shop. It's going to take time, Toby. There is a lot more to be found in San Francisco."

"That's okay. We make a start. I want to sleep with Jared in his home. *Tonight.*" Toby's mouth firmed, inflexible. He looked to Sahara Blue, who had his muscular arms crossed, staring at Toby with what very much looked like admiration. "I need you on clean-up detail," Toby said. "Like me, you don't have much of a sense of the aesthetic." Sahara coughed in amusement at Toby's dry tone. "But you can hire someone to clean up the mess and replace the windows and appliances. Also, bathroom duty. New towels. You know he—"

Jai squeezed Toby's shoulder. "Take a breath."

"He loves bright colors, bath sheets rather than towels. Get them," Toby finished, grateful for the support. Why had he assumed that if he came out, he'd be alone, except for Jared? These two men stood with them.

"I also thought I'd gather all the stuff that is washing up around the wharf. Jared's shredded clothing mainly. And I can snorkel down to the bottom, see if I can find some of his stones and stuff," Sahara offered.

"Thank you, Sahara," Toby said. "It would be distressing for him to see his... his personal stuff in the drink like that." Thrown away like garbage. Toby felt grief and rage warring inside him. But right now he had to work on building again, not on anger, except for the anger that gave him courage.

There was another knock on the door but this time Toby blinked, looking at the others. Sahara shook his head, signaling he had no idea who it was this early in the morning.

When he opened the door, Ellen from makeup strode in. She crushed Toby in a hug. "Where's Jared?" she asked, looking around, her hair swinging softly against her face, her vividly made up face tight with outrage.

Toby had to clear his throat again. "Resting."

"Good, that's good. So what do you need us to do?"

"Us?" Toby stared at Ellen, seeing her pulling a note pad out of her bulky bag.

"Yeah. Us on the soap. We want to help you guys out."

Toby's lips quirked, rubbing the tight muscles on the back of his neck ruefully. "So it's out about me and Jared being a thing."

"Yeah, sorry. Is that a problem?" Ellen asked.

Toby shook his head. "No. It might have been yesterday, but not today." Jared had given him plenty of opportunities to return to his safe path, but now he was well and truly out. Let anyone who didn't like it squawk. He was through being the easygoing guy who lived with an ache in his gut.

"I'm glad something good came out of this," Ellen said. "So, what can we do for you? Gopher work? Clean up? Any errands we can help with?"

"Ellen, you guys making the offer is the best thing. The best thing. Thank you," Toby said. "Sahara had a lot to do. Can you coordinate with him?"

"Sure thing." She gave Sahara a smile, which he returned.

Toby had to turn away then, dazed. So much had happened in a short time. His turning to Jared, leaving the security of his girlfriend, his boring but predictable life, to experience his first sexual explorations with Jared, and then coming out. Was what had happened to Jared, the violation of his home, a direct result of that? Toby swallowed, not wanting to think about it right now. What mattered was they weren't alone.

He and Jared had each other. But they also had friends, sympathy, and support.

As he looked toward Jared's home, he thought maybe they had something else. Courage. Because they'd need that too.

"HOW are you feeling, sweetheart?" he asked Jared softly, sitting next to him in Sahara Blue's bed with a cup of steaming green tea. Jai had prepared it specially, and it reminded Toby rather poignantly of the night before, their wonderful date in the garden.

It seemed like a dream after what had happened: brutal reality.

Jared blinked, swallowing. His eyes were still red-rimmed, crusty from the tears he'd shed silently during the night while Toby held him, not letting go.

"I've been better," he croaked. But then he reached out for the green tea and pressed a kiss against Toby's lips. "You called me 'sweetheart'."

Toby colored. "Yep. Is that all right? I mean, between men?"

"Why not between men?" Jared asked, a lazy hand combing through Toby's hair.

"Okay then." Toby gave a small smile. "Can you be ready to go out in a little while?"

Jared looked at him out of dull eyes. Toby could see he was purposely avoiding the view of his vandalized house, or he'd spot a crew from the soap opera with brooms or a vacuum cleaner, making way for a 24-hour glazier, who was in to measure the windows. He'd promised Toby he'd have them in there by this afternoon, though it would be a big job. One of the producers from *Mission Bay* was picking up the tab for that.

A wet head popped up like a harbor seal: Sahara Blue. He was combing the sea floor for anything that could be salvaged of Jared's treasures. Already he'd removed the floating debris from his house, so Toby felt safe in escorting his boyfriend to his car, which fortunately hadn't been touched. Toby was grateful for that since Jared was fragile right now.

"Out where?"

"Shopping for our new home."

Jared's eyes widened. He put down the green tea with a rap on the bedside table. "*Our?* Toby—"

"I told you my intentions are honorable." Toby swallowed. "I fully intend to pursue you, Jared Asche, until we live together."

"You do?" A faint spark in Jared's eyes.

"Damn right. I have been moving in this direction, slowly, for a long time." Toby cleared his throat, hoping to reach through Jared's apathy. It hurt him to see him so demoralized. He'd always been so serene about who he was, but now Toby could see that the rituals he lived and his home had played a big part in grounding Jared.

Toby had to give it back to him.

"It's time to take action, to build something together."

"But what if...." Jared's voice trailed off, and pain flashed in his eyes.

What if I lose it again? What if it's taken from me?

"I can't promise you that someone won't try to hurt you—*us*— again, but we'll take steps this time to try to take better care of your house. Sahara Blue is going to take charge of the security for it this time. It won't be an easy mark."

"It hurts," Jared said. "I'm not sure how I can adjust to new stuff. It'll just seem—new. Not mine. And yet at the same time, I know I have to do my part. I have to get it together since I'm so lucky to have all of you to care about me, to help me out."

"The stuff won't seem quite like yours for a while, no." Toby reached out, gripped Jared's hand. "Give yourself time."

"Time is something I didn't offer you. I'm sorry your first time was so—"

Now Toby was on surer ground. He fisted his hand in Jared's dark, silky hair, holding him still while he gave him an aching kiss. "Don't be sorry," he whispered.

THEY started with the bedroom.

Toby opened the shop door of an Indian antique store Jai had recommended and breathed in the smell of teak oil and cardamom. Now this seemed like Jared's kind of place.

He gripped Jared's arm gently as they stood at the entrance, taking in the ambiance. He waited, watching him.

Jared took a deep breath and then looked at Toby.

"It was worth it."

"Huh?" Toby blinked, not following his new lover's thought.

"Losing everything. To have you; it was worth it," Jared said. "Just wanted you to know."

Toby nodded, afraid he'd get emotional again when they had shit to do. "Okay," he whispered. "Do you see anything you like here?"

"Yeah, that bed." Jared pointed toward a carved high platform with painted wood and twining flowers and vegetables etched. It was a total fantasy bed, not something that Toby would ever have considered.

The store clerk intercepted them, smiling, "That is used to deliver an Indian bride to her wedding."

Jared chewed his lip. "Maybe some gauzy curtains, like mosquito netting." He looked at the clerk. "Can you fit it out with a mattress?"

And then Toby took a shaky breath.

It would be okay. Maybe. They were taking an important first step, moving away from the shards of Jared's former home and building a new one.

Jared suddenly turned around and new uncertainty clouded his brown eyes, something Toby was unused to seeing. "You like it?"

"Yes. It's very you."

"But I thought you wanted a place for both of us?"

"Jared, that would be a hotplate on the floor and a TV, if it were left to me." He gave a little laugh, squeezing Jared's hand.

Jared laughed back and shook his head. "Right. What was I thinking?"

On the way to their next destination, Toby driving since Jared was still a little shaken; they passed an artisan's street stands, out for the weekend. Toby was amazed it was Saturday. Last he remembered, it was Thursday, before their big date and the night they'd crashed to earth.

"Stop!"

He tensed, studying Jared's face.

Jared reached over and cupped the back of his neck, massaging, a touch of his old self back in place as he showed his care and concern for his new partner. "I want to pick something up for my... our place. Is that all right?"

Toby kept his face impassive at the question. He knew that Jared would get his balance back. "Anything you want," he said.

Toby watched as Jared chose from what looked like silk scarves to him, rippling with creases like undulating waves. He caught some phrases, like *Delos pleats,* but didn't understand what Jared had in mind for the material until Jared put his arm around Toby. "Tablecloths and an altar cloth for, um...." His face darkened and Toby knew he was remembering his lost Kwan Yin.

"Jai suggested a place to look for one," Toby said, reaching up to cup Jared's cheek. He was suddenly conscious of a couple of onlookers staring as they walked past the two of them, and it occurred to Toby he was being openly affectionate with his boyfriend in public again.

"I may not find her the first try," Jared warned, sighing. "And I don't even want to think of my instruments."

"So don't," Toby suggested. "You weren't playing recently anyway, on one of your natural breaks. When you are moved to play again, you'll find something right or even borrow a mandolin from one of your musician friends. Don't they have some old ones lying around? You did."

Jared blinked. "Yeah, I could do that." His voice sounded more and more like himself. He looked at Toby and added softly, "Thanks, sweetheart."

At an Asian antiques store, Jared paused, looking inside through the window. He shook his head but Toby took his arm. "Let's just have a look around."

"I don't see her."

"No, and you won't. But now maybe you need a new lady in your life. Jared, what happened to you... you need to fall back on all your rituals to try to heal. I know you. I know you can do this, since you did it for me."

Jared looked at Toby with more assurance. "I did that for you, really?"

"How could I resist you? Your incense and your sexy body and the way you handled me." Toby's voice lowered to a pleasurable growl as he reminisced. "I remember that first sex scene we had to do. Me sitting on your lap, your hands on my bare ass. I remember getting this weird, charged feeling at the way you touched me: you were confident, appreciative, like you were so comfortable with another man's body. From under my shell, that was enticing."

Jared pushed open the door and they walked inside. Now Toby could see curiosity in his eyes and not sickness. He felt his shoulders relax a little and let Jared do a circuit of the room. He didn't care what Jared brought home, if anything. Whatever it was, it would be right because *Jared* chose it.

He believed in him, even if Jared's faith in himself was a little wobbly.

His BlackBerry buzzed, and he answered the call, nodding with satisfaction as Sahara Blue outlined what had been accomplished. Then his eyes widened as he heard of Jai's gift. "Wow," he told Sahara.

"Yep."

"Can he…?"

"Jai is pretty well off, I think. He's in a lucrative industry," Sahara joked.

"Okay." It didn't even cause him a flicker of concern now, Jai giving to them. He guessed they'd gone through the fire, but, as a result, he felt closer to Jared now. Everything else felt trivial.

"That's pretty special. And Sahara, for your gift—thank you."

"I want to dance at your wedding," Sahara teased. Or was he teasing? Toby blushed and was glad the other man couldn't see it as he ended the call.

In the end, it was easy, finding their new goddess.

She was taller than the other one, about five feet in height, made of carved wood, and she was worn and cracked. She had a warm, light gold finish, and her expression seemed a little gentler, more content, as if she knew she was going to a secure new home.

"She's been made to look like that, a replica," Jared said, as if feeling the need to be critical. It wasn't like him.

"I like her," Toby said.

"Yeah?"

"Yeah."

"We'll take her," Jared said, offering his credit card.

The proprietor shook his head. "It has been taken care of, Sir. Anything you wanted today."

Jared looked at Toby.

"Jai," Toby said. He pulled out his own worn leather wallet and put a hunk of a gold crystal on the counter. "I'll buy this."

Jared picked it up, studying it. "It's citrine. Supposed to bring fortune to a home."

"We don't need it," Toby said. "But I'd like it somewhere."

Jared was running his hands over it. "Maybe the kitchen. It would be nice in the windowsill—it would pick up the light."

"Sure," Toby said.

Jared narrowed one eye. "What other surprises have you and Sahara and Jai cooked up?"

Toby grinned. There was anticipation in Jared's voice.

"I guess we'll have to go home now to see for ourselves, and then head out for a good meal."

"I feel like sushi," Jared said, rubbing his stomach which Toby knew had been upset earlier. "Something light. But first we need to make one more stop."

Toby raised his brows. "For?"

"A couple of special toys for my boy," Jared growled. "And I still want to spank your ass."

Toby's body hardened in response. Spanking. Oh, yeah, he could get into that.

Chapter 21

SAHARA BLUE was tired and sun burnt, but he had a pleasant feeling of accomplishment from helping Jared and Toby. He peeled out of his wet suit vest and then, acting on compulsion, tapped a few keys on his laptop computer.

Maybe Lotus had answered him. Stranger things had happened. And he'd commented to him again, after the fragment of the story Lotus had put up the other night. They'd had a little online spat about it:

You're not going to leave it there. I want the rest, Sahara had posted on Lotus's blog.

So bossy. I suppose you're an impatient man, Lotus had replied, somewhat snarky to Sahara's sense.

I'm impatient for you, he shot back baldly. *I want you.*

That story isn't about me, not really. It's just something I made up.

It is you, Sahara said.

Now as he logged on, he discovered that Lotus had written another installment, days earlier than his once-a-week habit. Because Sahara had pushed him? Heat moved through him at the thought. "Son of a bitch," he muttered, leaning close to read, lips parted in anticipation.

Early on, my owner confronted me with a strange apparatus in a glass tank. All the metal probes and leather buckles made me a little apprehensive, so I struggled for the first time when he tried to put me inside it.

Firmly, he held me until I relaxed, rubbing my bare back. Then he placed me inside the tank which had two areas near the floor that were open, like windows. He used those as access to buckle me inside it, perching me in a position suspended by the metal prongs so that my ass was raised high and my face against the tank floor. My legs were spread and my ankles and wrists buckled firmly.

My cock hung free, hard and pulsing.

Once I was strapped in, he lifted the tank and placed it by what I'd nicknamed his "comfy" chair in front of an entertainment screen. He liked to relax there in the evenings, sometimes with me chained on the floor. He was in the habit of using me as a footrest, running his feet over my arching spine. It was an oddly pleasurable ritual for both of us.

Now he pressed a button on the side of the tank, and I heard something mechanical start up. A cold metal probe pushed inside of me and I shuddered, tensing.

My owner was watching his programs, ignoring me.

Emollient shot out of the probe, making me slick. The thin metal prod pulled out but a second later I was penetrated by a bulbous shape. Suspended as I was, I was helpless to shift my body at all. Sweat broke out on my forehead and my armpits as the bulb inside tapped against my prostate directly.

My cock dripped precum, and finally I made a soft sound, my erection hanging heavy, so needy.

And my owner reached into the tank where I was imprisoned and fondled me, playing with my hanging sex in an absent fashion, as if handling a pet.

The slow fucking continued, so that I strained toward the silver probe entering me, desperate for any edge of stimulation.

Now and then my owner petted me, exploring my cock and balls thoroughly and affectionately.

At first I thought it was torture, pure torture, but then I had a new idea; he was training me.

"Shit!" Sahara snarled, stumbling away from his desk chair, sweating, hard, and pissed off. Damn Lotus was *teasing* him!

He squeezed his eyes shut, picturing taking the minx in hand, perhaps tying him up and then doing teasing similar to that of the owner and his pet in Lotus's futuristic fantasy.

Knowing he was due over at Jared's floating home for his all important homecoming soon, Sahara typed out one pithy phrase to Lotus in answer to his continued story:

I'm going to have you.

TOBY leaned against Jared as they left his car behind them. Jared's arm was thrown casually around him in a way that just a few days ago Toby would have been uncomfortable with in public.

Now he felt a kind of awareness but no shame.

Everything else had fallen away; when Jared had lost everything, it had been like he'd lived that experience with him and seen his lover reduced. And in the end, Jared had been all that mattered.

"I can't believe the stuff we picked up today!" Jared was saying, looking slightly uneasy. "It seemed so... impulsive."

"Not impulsive. What happened to you was fast, torn away from you, so maybe it calls for a little fast action in response. Stuff will settle."

Jared nodded, nuzzling Toby, his face unshaven and a little dangerous-looking with his beard shadow, his warm brown eyes fixed on Toby's face. "Well, the moon will be in Taurus soon, so that is about the basics, about focusing on what is most important."

Toby laughed. "Okay, then." He shook his head. He and Jared had nothing in common. Except maybe what was most important.

JARED tensed when he saw who was sitting outside his deck that fronted the entrance to his house. The cop, Martinez, and a familiar woman, Tina, who had tumbling dark hair and wore a tie-dyed T-shirt. They were sipping drinks from a jug provided by Sahara Blue, whose nose was freshly reddened from too much sun.

Knowing the reason for that, that he had spent most of the day in the water retrieving Jared's possessions according to Toby, Jared squeezed Sahara's shoulder as he passed him. "Hey."

"Hey back. You and Toby want some of my custom-blend Sangria?" Sahara made it with Tabasco sauce and real Brandy and oranges. It had a helluva kick.

"Sure, I think that would go down nicely." The burn of the alcohol would make it easier to take in his home, the changes he was apprehensive about seeing, touching, like a wound that still seeped, raw. But he'd only have one glass and make sure both of the other men stopped there too. He had plans for later that didn't mix well with alcohol.

Sahara poured him and Toby short glasses, as if guessing at Jared's intentions while Tina leaned forward, touching his arm. "I'm sorry about the heron door," she said. "Damn, it was one of my favorite creations!"

"So am I," Jared said, looking at his temporary plywood door. "You really did a nice job on it."

"Well, I am working a lot more with stained glass as well as etched glass now, so I'd like to discuss some design possibilities with you now. Maybe I can sketch something out." Tina had a pad with her and opened it, showing some colorful examples to Jared that made his eyes widen. Then his eyes fell on a stained glass door depicting a merman seducing a sailor.

"Oh yeah. That!"

Tina laughed. "Shall I give the sailor blond hair?" She nodded to Toby, who was sitting close to Jared.

Jared smiled at his new partner, remembering all he'd done to take care of him when he'd felt so brittle. He'd be rewarding his boy, oh yes.

Toby held his hand as he stepped inside his home for the first time since he'd left it in pieces.

It smelled pleasantly of furniture polish and rose potpourri. There was a pink salt crystal sconce on the new coffee table, which was made out of a recycled door from India. He and Toby had picked it out from the same shop as the new bed.

The couch, a turquoise color with microfiber, had been delivered, but the room was scant of much other furniture yet. Tatami mats took the place of the shredded Persian ones that Jared had once owned.

The kitchen was tidy, plates from Portugal sitting stacked on the corner, fresh from a run in the dishwasher. Jared walked over and brushed the new state of the art stainless steel appliances, all geared for low water and power, which suited his home. "Wow."

"Jai bought them for you. And the door will be a gift from Sahara, once Tina makes it," Toby said.

"I'm glad that this time with the cameras and built in security system, my home will be safer," Jared said. He'd sat down earlier with Sahara and gone over a concise home security plan that even caught the approval of Officer Martinez, who had kindly dropped by to make sure Jared's new home would be more secure.

"I'M SORRY it's necessary to take those steps," Toby added, thinking that the time would come soon when he'd been dealing with whoever might have vandalized Jared's home. He planned to handle that on his own and spare his new lover any more pain. The idea that this attack might have been inspired by him....

He had to push away the thought, the sickness it brought to his gut. Refocus on Jared and his tentative new steps through his redone home.

At the bedroom, Jared took in the pristine bed they'd chosen with a single combination mattress and box spring made up in saffron silk bedding. The new Kwan Yin sat at rest by the windows looking out at the harbor, a scattering of recovered crystals surrounding her like a glittering rainbow.

On the floor by the bed was something Toby had bought Jared and he watched Jared go over and kneel beside it. "I've wanted one of these nebulizers since I first saw one," Jared noted, a shy smile lighting his face.

Beautiful. He was so beautiful when he was radiant like that, Toby thought.

"I know," Toby said smugly, watching water and essential oil mist the air with the soothing scent of lavender and oranges, the machine turning color, purple to green to red to blue and all the soft shades in between. "I thought it would be romantic in our room."

"Our room. I've never had an 'our room' before," Jared said, sitting on the hardwood floor and looking out at the serene view through the newly replaced windows—they also offered a new touch; a seagull frieze etched out at the top of each panel.

Toby settled behind Jared, opening his legs and encompassing his man's larger body, feeling the throb of want, so he knew that Jared had to feel his cock pushing insistently against his backside.

After a moment, face almost sober, Jared turned around and reached into Toby's loose silk pants, which he'd changed into for comfort over at Sahara's after their day of shopping.

Jared helped himself to Toby's erection, stroking him as Toby shuddered and his head fell back, giving himself completely to Jared.

"I think we better take care of this, don't you?" Jared asked, raising a brow.

"Yes, Jared," Toby whispered. "Please."

SAHARA BLUE was in the great room, waiting for them, having seen Tina back to her car.

Jared told him, "Take Toby's clothes off and shave him clean." Jared settled on some pillows to watch and Toby caught his breath as Sahara's fingers opened his shirt, peeling it aside so his nipples puckered from the slight chill in the room, brought on by it being open for a good part of a day and a night.

Sahara was efficient, eyes down, handling Toby kindly but firmly. He tugged Toby's pants off his monster erection, leaving him naked and exposed to both men's eyes.

"Stand there," Sahara ordered.

Lips parted and color high in his cheeks, Toby waited as Sahara filled a warm bowl and retrieved new hand towels and shaving equipment. When Sahara returned, he knelt at Toby's feet and pushed his legs wider for better access.

Heart pounding, Toby held Jared's commanding gaze shyly as Sahara soaped him, stroking his cock, handling him as Jared's surrogate.

Then there was the rasp of the razor over slick flesh, Toby standing perfectly still as Sahara prepared him for Jared. When it was finally done to Jared and Sahara's satisfaction, Sahara patted him dry tenderly.

Jared tossed a sack he'd picked up at the toy store in Sahara's direction. "Tie his wrists with the spun bamboo rope in front of him. Nothing fancy."

Sahara made a humming sound of pleasure as he handled the rope, which was a bright white color, almost luminescent in the dim light. "Nice and light, and I've heard its machine washable," he praised as he tied Toby's hands.

Toby felt the way he had in the attic room of Jared's, like a beautiful object.

"You remember your safe word, boy?" Sahara asked him, tapping his bare thigh to get his attention.

"Yes, Sahara," Toby said, feeling powerful and sexy, submissive, but their submissive.

Both men escorted him to the bedroom where Sahara had placed a large pillow on the center of the bed.

"Climb on there so your bottom is raised," Jared ordered Toby, his confidence potent, restored by his lover and his friends so he and Toby could play again. "Sahara will assist you since your hands are tied. Make yourself comfortable and take some deep breaths. When I'm ready, I'm going to spank you."

Sahara did help Toby, taking care of him as if he was precious. When he was positioned, his ass was high and he waited, lips parted, panting.

"I'm going to make that ass nice and pink and Sahara is going to stay here and watch as my boy gets spanked," Jared growled. "Like that idea?"

Toby's toes curled. He rubbed his wet-tipped cock hard against the silk pillow.

"Yes, Jared," he whispered, holding Jared's gaze, wildly aware of how he was positioned naked on the bed while the other two men were clothed and in possession of him.

"Yes, Jared, what?" Jared raised a cool brow, kneeling behind Toby.

"Yes, Jared, spank my ass," Toby said.

Chapter 22

"JARED." Toby didn't know what he was asking for, holding Jared's gaze, but Jared seemed to have a sense of what was simmering between them, rising like one of his favorite erotic incenses.

He knelt on the bed behind Toby and held out his hand next to Toby's face. Sahara got on the other side, running a stroking hand over Toby's bare back and rear end so he shivered, stimulated.

Toby nuzzled the dark hairs on the back of Jared's hand with parted lips, aroused at what was about to happen, aroused at being handled by both men like a beautiful possession. He'd never felt sexier in his life. And his throat tightened as he thought that if he hadn't had the courage to go for this, to pursue Jared, he never would have experienced this.

He closed his eyes and kissed the back of Jared's hand and heard him catch his breath. "You make this—" Jared's voice was tight. "Toby, it's different with someone I love. You made me strong today."

"I love you strong," Toby said, smiling into the mirror and Jared's brown eyes. Eyes that had guided him, watched him; eyes he had been conscious of for many months now, focused in his direction. Anita had been right; he'd loved that Jared had a thing for him.

"I'm going to spank you because it will be a pleasure to see your ass grow pink, to watch the expressions on your face," Jared outlined, caressing Toby's back. "Toby, I rarely take anyone this far."

Toby shivered. "I belong to you."

Jared and Sahara caressed him, murmuring to him about how beautiful he was, how smooth his skin, how sexy he looked. His cock was heavy between his legs, and he rubbed it shamelessly against the pillow as he squirmed, lifting up to their touch.

The spanking was more prolonged and gentle to begin with than he'd imagined. Jared's hand was cupped, fingers together, so the smacks were loud in the quiet of the room. Toby felt like he was getting into a really hot bath, moving from tingling to slightly stinging. He was immersed in the experience, the irregular tattoo of a palm hitting his flesh, the caught breath of his caregiver's.

Jared paused, watching him like a hawk. He could see Sahara also watching him, a peculiar mixture of arousal and appreciation and attention on his face. He was enjoying watching Toby get his ass spanked while his hands were tied, giving Toby the feeling of being helpless, even as he reached over often, checking Toby's balance, touching him and stroking Toby's warming rear end. He was a natural guardian, like Jared.

Jared reached down and helped Toby on his hands and knees so he could explore Toby's sex. Toby gasped since the sensations seemed magnified now with his glowing ass. There was something about being groped as his rear-end flushed with color.

A moment later, Jared resumed, smacking Toby slightly harder and making him grunt, sweat breaking out on his forehead. It stung a little, but strangely, Toby wanted to push up into the sting, craving the sensation as he watched himself spanked and groped in the mirror, emphasizing his sexy submission to these two special men.

He panted when Jared struck him again harder, this time with an open hand so it really bloomed. And again. "Oh God, Jared!" He needed—

"Sahara will help you sit up, boy." Jared caressed Toby's warmed ass appreciatively, like it was a work of art he'd painted on flesh.

Sahara lifted him, and without his support, Toby might have flopped awkwardly. He was trembling.

"Sahara," he moaned to Sahara when he also helped himself to Toby's erection, stroking it, groping him while Jared watched.

Jared sat back on his knees while Sahara continued to tease Toby, never giving him enough touch to get off until Toby was moaning, thrusting wantonly toward Sahara's hand like a tame bird.

Jared gave a small nod to Sahara, and Sahara took Toby's cock firmly in hand, giving him a fast hand job.

"What about it, slut?" he asked gently.

"Please, Sahara," Toby gasped. "Please, Jared, let me come!"

Jared gave him a smack on the rear and then he was coming, coming in Sahara's fist while Jared also caressed him, encouraging him, owning him. He could see his surrender played out in the mirror, his contorted face, his arching body, his prick in Sahara's possession.

After he spurted, Sahara used a damp towel he had on hand to cleanse him, very gently, since Toby was wildly sensitive. He gasped, but allowed it. *He was theirs.*

Finally Sahara let him lie down against the pillow again, where he lay gasping, recovering.

In the reflection from the mirror, he saw Jared reach into the bedside drawer and pull out some lube.

Toby remembered his first time with Jared. It had been overwhelming, powerful. But he felt so relaxed right now, almost floating, his body heavy with satiation. He felt inviting, like the slut Sahara had called him.

Jared's eyes remained on his face as he anointed his fingers. He pushed them inside Toby and Toby gave a long groan as Jared immediately stroked his prostrate.

"My boy needs to be fucked," Jared whispered tenderly.

"Yes," Toby whispered.

Sahara smiled, looking as content as Toby was. He winked at Toby and then left him alone with Jared.

Huffing, Toby was more than ready to be fucked when he felt the brush of open denim against his thighs and then the warm prod of Jared's cock, pushing against his entrance.

Jared paused to rub a hand over Toby's pink ass. "You're a beautiful sex toy."

When he thrust inside Toby, Toby's head fell back and his fingers clenched. He was still bound, and it made it seem sexier to him. But he'd never felt more grounded. Swaying forward, he held Jared's eyes in the mirror, and saw the pleasure on his man's face.

"I love you so much," Toby croaked. "When you were hurting…."

"You made me not hurt," Jared finished poignantly. Tears simmered suddenly in his eyes as he bent close to Toby and kissed the side of his face. "I love you. My beautiful slut, I love you."

Rocking slowly, Toby was mesmerized by the flexible play of their shadows against the other side of the bedroom wall. The moment that Jared grabbed him, arms around him, groaning, dying inside Toby, Toby watched, rapt.

SAHARA BLUE took a sip of his microwave heated coffee, knocking back the exhaustion of the long day, but he wasn't going to fall asleep now, no sir.

He had done his best, with some input from Officer Martinez—who was cute and maybe Sahara had glimpsed a spark of interest in his eyes?—to make sure that his friends would be safe tonight, but for some reason, watching all the activity, he'd had an itchy feeling all day at the back of his neck, like they were all being observed.

He'd looked around, but the harbor was circled by lots of historic buildings, lots of places for people to park and watch from a distance. Still, he couldn't shake the idea that someone was out there, the person who had hurt Jared by violating his home. Waiting for a chance to do it again, only this time it would be worse, because it was the fragile new creation that Jared and Toby were making together.

Sahara Blue would be damned if it would happen again.

So he sipped his coffee on his deck and kept a sharp eye out. He could sleep in the morning.

JARED turned over and put an arm around Toby, watching as Toby stared at the steam rising from the scent dispenser, the colors changing, hypnotic, green to amber to yellow to pink to purple to blue and over again. It was the only light in his—*their* room.

"I like it," he said, rubbing his whiskered chin gently against the back of Toby's neck so his lover shivered and then laughed.

"I probably would have bought it for you even if we weren't... you know."

"You were a good friend," Jared acknowledged.

"I'm a better lover," Toby said smugly. He turned over to face Jared and they both stared at each other, getting used to sharing a bed, to the intimacy of talking in one after making love.

They'd shared a tub bath after their sex, rinsing off in the shower first, Jared holding a wobbly Toby gently, and then lying in the heated water, not speaking, just touching, finding reassurance, finding something solid.

"I have to go and see Mike tomorrow," Toby said soberly. "After what happened.... I can't put it off anymore though I wish to fuck I could."

"No," Jared said, automatic.

"Jared!"

Jared scrubbed his jaw. "It's too soon," he almost pleaded. Toby had been under that man's thumb for years. What if he walked away because of Mike? Jared's gut tightened. "We haven't had any time together, Tobes."

"I know that," Toby said, earnest. He reached out and nested his fingers through Jared's. "Don't you think I know that? I hate that things have pushed us, and yet, maybe it was a good thing."

"Because you would have been afraid of coming out to your parents and Anita?"

Toby nodded, swallowing. "I can't help that I wish they'd be proud of me. It's always hurt, the way Mike was constantly running me down." His jaw hardened. "But it doesn't have to be that way. I have made up my mind to be my own man."

"I like your own man," Jared teased, reaching up to cup Toby's face, knowing Toby had to see his concern.

Toby grinned. "I know you do. I never felt better about sex in my life!" He stretched, and the lines of his arching body, tangled blond hair, unshaven, sleepy blue eyes, beautiful skin with white blond hair coating the backs of his arms.

"That's good," Jared said, knowing his eyes were heavy and suggestive.

Toby leaned close and kissed him. "It hasn't been a typical sexual courtship, but it's been pretty special. Thank you."

"You're special." Feeling how he was becoming emotional, as he was still fragile from what had happened to his home, Jared took a deep breath. He didn't want to dwell on dark things right now. He wanted to lie, consoled, at home, in Toby's arms.

He buried his face against Toby's neck, and Toby put his arms around him, their erections brushing softly under the sheet. He rolled on top of Toby and Toby's hands clenched over his covered ass, kneading it pleasurably.

"Want to know what I want to do now?" Toby asked archly.

"What?" Jared raised an amused brow.

"Maybe watch a little *Chuck*, get baked, but first...." Toby slid suggestively against Jared and then reached down to touch his erection. Jared lifted off slightly to the side.

"Take us both in hand, Toby."

Toby wet his lips, encompassing them both in his hand, his eyes wide at yet another new experience.

Jared felt anchored to the bed by his merman; when they did come, it would be quick, like a candle blowing out. And he recognized Toby was asking for some of the comfortable rituals they'd shared as friends for so long with the movie—because he intended to confront his family the next day.

"I want to go with you," he said huskily, bending close to touch his lips against Toby's as Toby's working increased speed. Oh yeah!

"No, Jared. I don't want that for you."

"Hey, you don't have to be so protective of me. Thanks to you, I feel like myself again." Jared leaned his forehead against Toby's damp one, panting now. He was so close but enjoying hovering near the flame. "I won't get into it."

Toby quirked a brow.

"Okay, not much. But I want to be there. Aren't we partners now?" he said the last softly.

"Working on it partners," Toby said, giving Jared stroke that made him arch his back, cry out. "See?"

DROWSY after, Jared opened his mouth to argue further but then shut it a moment later. Toby was his own man, and he wanted time to think it over.

Yet uneasiness moved through Jared's guts. If Mike had been the one to vandalize his home, what might he do to Toby?

He had to do something to protect Toby.

SAHARA had admittedly begun to feel damn sleepy since it was almost dawn, but this was also the most likely time for someone to strike again.

He stood up, shaking his arms and legs, seeing the red line on the horizon of the coming ball of sun. He'd take a little walk around the wharf; it would mean he could keep watch but it would also keep him alert.

TOBY looked over at Jared, who was slumped on his new couch, snoring. He was probably still really tired from the lack of sleep. Toby stroked his hair of his forehead, wishing that being with Jared hadn't resulted in hurting this man. It was the last thing he'd wanted.

He got up and walked to the floor to ceiling windows, looking out at the lightening sky, the color of gunmetal now. He traced one of the orca frieze figures at the top of the new windows. He was glad Jared was embracing the changes, glad that a lot of them were the result of gifts so that the other man could feel how many people cared about him.

Toby grabbed his wallet, deciding he'd head out for a couple of wraps on the wharf for the two of them. Hell, they'd never even had dinner last night, but now he was starving, and Jared would be to as soon as he woke up.

He wanted to eat quickly so they could both get to the good stuff, more fooling around.

He shut the door behind him and then jumped at what he found waiting outside his new home.

SAHARA BLUE examined a good-sized rock he'd discovered on the wharf by Jared and Toby's home. Turns out he'd been right; someone had come here to make trouble. Sahara had missed the stalker but he must have frightened the person away, fortunately, most likely when he'd come out from behind the covered boathouses on the other side of the pier.

"Huh." Probably been planning to use it to shatter a window. Thinking how upsetting that would have been for his friends, Sahara was glad he'd stayed up all night, keeping a look out.

The plywood door creaked open and Toby stepped outside, blinking. He gaped at Sahara. "You're up early," he noted. "What have you got there?"

And Sahara dropped the rock, kicked it behind him, and raised his other find. "I don't know, I think he's abandoned."

Toby made a soft sound and a second later was cradling a heavy, sleepy puppy body, looking at the wrinkled face which was oddly flat, like it had been squished together. For some reason, he found that adorable.

"He's a mutt," Sahara said, thinking to himself that Jared was a goner. He'd soon have more than a new boyfriend.

Chapter 23

SAHARA BLUE made instant cereal and ate it from a chipped brown mug as he stood by his floor-to-ceiling windows. The food tasted like warmed wood chips to his tongue. He was eager to crash, get some sleep. He knew he couldn't do this every night, watch over Jared and Toby's place, but fortunately he thought he knew who might be behind it, after all. The person had made a mistake and left a possible clue.

He'd get some shuteye, and later on today he'd take care of business.

As he passed his study on the way to his bedroom, his laptop beeped.

Fresh email.

He paused, groaning, really tired but he couldn't ignore any contact with the alluring Lotus.

He went into the study, tapped a few keys and discovered that finally the comment he'd left the first time on the enigmatic man's blog had been answered.

He had written: *Are you as lonely as I am?*

Below his comment, Lotus has written: *I am very lonely.*

SETH HOLLIS swallowed thickly as he walked the cement wall looking over the small harbor, taking in the floating homes and moored boats. It hadn't been too difficult for him to find Sahara Blue—he was in the phone book. Had he wanted to lure Lotus into looking for him? Well, if so, he'd succeeded. Increasingly, Seth felt constrained by his online persona. He wanted something else, but he was afraid to really go for it. It was much safer to put in time in his shop and then go upstairs as he did every night to eat, read, and sleep.

But he and Sahara lived pretty close to each other, as it turned out.

He caught a glimpse of a sandy-blond head and dark-tinted sunglasses that seemed to scan the wharf's surroundings from Sahara's floating home, and Seth dodged into the shadow of an alley, heart pounding.

What was he even doing here?

Except that Sahara had said he was lonely. And so was Seth.

JARED was parked outside of Mike and Lorraine Danvers' suburban home. He'd only been to this house, this neighborhood previously to pick up Toby on occasions when they were going to spend some time together or Toby needed a lift to work after visiting his family.

He rubbed his jaw, studying the bungalow and imagining Toby growing up here. He hadn't been a jock, or a brain; instead, he'd like doing landscaping for extra money. Mike Danvers had always ridden him to be more and do more, getting on Jared's nerves, though he'd kept it to himself. It hadn't been his place to speak up.

And Toby had tried, Jared knew. Tried for years to be what everyone wanted him to be, but his sadness had called to the protector in Jared as much as his hot body. Jared had always seemed to be the one to see Toby, find him sitting alone somewhere, like the occasion when he'd been sipping a beer on his birthday.

The memory of that now possessed a special poignancy. He ached for Toby's isolation that night, but it had also been the night that Toby'd shocked the hell out of Jared and kissed him.

The front door opened just then, and the man Jared had been thinking of stepped outside to pick up the daily newspaper. He stiffened as he took in Jared's distinctive baby blue DeSoto.

Jared got out of his car.

"DO YOU have a name for him?" Tina asked, taking precise measurements for the new door she would be crafting for him and Jared. It would be stained and etched glass, but it would also be metal and a little more sturdy than the first one.

Toby hefted up his chunky puppy, who hung over his hand limply. He was downy, floppy-eared, and long-bodied like a tan sausage, with big brown sad eyes that tugged at Toby's gut. "I thought maybe Albert, but I want, uh, Jared's input."

"Jared not in favor of a pet?" Ellen asked. She'd come over this morning as well, since she'd found a few more tag sale purchases for Jared's home. Toby adored the jeweled Buddha she'd brought, and he thought Jared would really go nuts over it. Ellen was getting cheesecake and coffee for that find at their favorite dessert place, and Toby had already reimbursed her for her purchases.

Toby shrugged. "He went for some pet food, but that doesn't mean we're adopting Albert."

"Is that what he told you?" Tina asked, giving Ellen an amused look.

"What?" Toby glared at both women. He was still sleepy, slow to follow them. Jared had left their place damn early on the errand for the puppy, which, okay, had already messed on their hardwood floor—twice—but Toby had cleaned it up.

Ellen's eyes softened. "Just that we both think if you want that puppy or, well, *anything,* Jared will find a way to get it for you."

Tina nodded. "You're lucky, Toby. He wanted this metal incorporated especially to offer extra protection for your front door. He really digs keeping you safe."

Toby blinked, a cold tingle running down his back. "Oh shit." He rubbed his whiskered jaw and handed the puppy to a surprised Ellen.

"What? Toby, what are you—?"

Toby shook his head, reaching for his wallet and the keys to the old Toyota he drove and had parked in Jared's extra rented space after they'd shifted some gear from the slot.

"You just said it," he said to Ellen before taking off toward the parking lot at a run. *That man would do anything for me.*

He was opening his car door when a hand grasped his wrist. He turned and looked into Sahara Blue's concerned blue eyes. He was so wound up, he didn't even blush at seeing him again, even after what they'd shared the night before. One name was twisting his gut.

Jared.

"I want to come with you," Sahara said.

"Jeez! I can handle this myself, I'm a big boy!"

"I have seen that for myself." Sahara was at the passenger side. Toby leaned over and opened the door, letting him in. He gave him a fierce look.

"Jared's gone off to deal with my stepfather."

Sahara nodded serenely. "Yeah, I figured that was where he was going."

"I don't need to be protected!" Toby fumed. Jared just thought he was stronger now, but Toby knew he was still recovering. He'd blink when he took in his home sometimes, still adjusting to the wrecking-ball that had struck his life.

"I'll stay in the car when you talk to your folks."

Toby swung grimly into traffic. He gave Sahara a suspicious look, not fooled at all by his air of innocence. "So why come then?"

"I have an errand," Sahara said.

"Hmmmm." But he dismissed his friend from his mind, ranging ahead, worrying. If Mike had been behind what had happened to

Jared's place…. No, it was unbearable. For all the difficulties he and Mike had had, Toby loved him.

He hadn't been able to let himself delve too deeply into who had hurt Jared, because he knew he didn't want to know the answer.

It had to be someone Toby cared about.

When he pulled up, he saw Jared leaning against his distinctive DeSoto, arms crossed. Mike Danvers was talking to him, hands on his hips.

Shit!

Ignoring Sahara, Toby flung open his car door and sprinted toward the two men.

Mike blinked when Toby was suddenly standing between his stepfather and his new boyfriend.

"Where'd you come from?"

"Home."

"You mean with *him*?"

Toby took a deep breath, steadying himself.

At the same time, Jared pushed away from the car, looking like he wanted to pull Toby close, protective, but hesitating because he probably feared Toby might not be comfortable with a gesture like that in front of his stepfather.

Toby shook his head, glowering at both men. "Mike, all your dire predictions came true: I'm gay."

Mike held Toby's defiant gaze.

Jared shrugged, as if to say *well, you've done it now,* and put an arm around Toby. Toby's tense shoulders immediately relaxed a little at Jared's magic touch.

"I didn't want this for you," Mike said softly, not riding Toby right off the way he'd expected. "I just can't understand it. It has to be *him.*" He glared at Jared. "I told him to leave you alone more than once."

"It was him," Toby said, face feeling like a mask over the shaking feeling inside. "He gave me the courage to be the man I always have been."

"If he had just left you alone…"

"Is that why you tore up his home, Dad?" Toby asked, tears pricking his eyes. *Oh God. Mike, how could you?*

"Tore up his…? The hell?" Mike shook his head, looking confused. "I don't even know where the hell he lives!"

"Come on, you wrecked his home. You just admitted telling him to leave me alone! How could you? His place was… it made me sick, seeing what you did. Sick and ashamed."

Mike prodded Toby's chest with a stiff finger. "I didn't do anything to your—" He swallowed, obviously cutting off a word. "Your friend. All I've done for months is warn him to stay away from you, and I did it again just now."

Toby looked to Jared and Jared nodded quietly. "He loves you, Toby, in his own way."

"I don't need you to speak for me!" Mike growled.

Jared remained silent, but his mouth tightened.

"You didn't wreck Jared's place…." Toby's voice trailed off. And then he went with his heart and pulled away from Jared, and hugged Mike.

Mike was stiff and silent, but he didn't push Toby away. After a moment, Toby pulled back. "I guess you're disappointed in me, but this is how it is from now on."

"I wish it wasn't," Mike said. He turned away but then hesitated. With his back to Toby, he said. "I always worried about you, Toby, so goddamned much."

Toby's throat tightened as the only father he'd ever known returned to the house where he'd grown up.

He took a deep breath and then looked at Jared. "I'm so glad it wasn't him."

"Me too," Jared said very gently. "And maybe…."

"Maybe." Toby wasn't sure. But Mike hadn't said never to call or come by again. "All this time, him railing on me was because he actually...."

"Cares about you, yeah." Jared agreed. "Let Sahara take your car, and we'll go back to the house in mine. Besides, we need to get some pet stuff and find a good vet. And more wipes. Your dog has a pretty active bladder."

"Oh, he's my dog?" Toby asked, letting Jared lighten up the moment a little.

"When he pees on my floor, he is," Jared said.

In the car, Toby squeezed his eyes shut, taking a shaking breath and then another.

Jared reached over and squeezed his hand. "I love you, Toby Rafferty."

Toby lifted Jared's hand and kissed the back of it.

"WHERE'D Sahara go? He didn't take the turn toward the docks." Toby got out of Jared's car, immediately recognizing where they were. It was where he'd taken Jared on that wonderful first date, to declare his intentions. They'd come full circle now.

"Who knows with him." Jared shrugged. He pulled Toby close, cupping the back of his head. "Right now you are my concern. Doing that with Mike was tough, painful, but he had to know who you are. Maybe with some time...."

Toby heaved out a sigh. "Okay, but I feel all bruised up."

"I'm sorry you had to do that." Jared didn't let go, but he did pull away so they could walk side by side toward the doorkeeper of the garden. The man's eyes widened, as if he recognized them. He took the bills Jared offered for admittance to the park and bowed as they passed him.

"We can't stay here too long. Puppy duty. Or maybe you think we should take the dog to the pound?"

"I think the dog was ours the moment Sahara put him into your arms," Jared noted dryly.

Toby brightened. He'd wanted a dog again so much, but his apartment was too small. This time it should work out; the puppy would have both of them, so that when he wasn't home, Jared might be.

"See? Look at that face," Jared said, settling with Toby near the Koi pond, where the rough grasses shifted softly against each other in the breeze. Toby could immediately feel his tension and upset slowly eroding, seeping in the peace of the garden, the peace of being with Jared. "No way I could resist making you look like that, like a sun rising over the water."

"Very poetic," Toby said.

Jared put an arm around him and they sat there, watching the aggressive fish, white and orange or flame colored or black as they shuffled through the water in search of food.

"If it wasn't Mike...." Toby didn't want to go back to the shadows right now, but they did need some finality to the question of who had vandalized Jared's home.

"Another day, Tobes."

"But—"

"These past few days you've made a commitment to me, moved in, and helped me rebuild my life. And just now you came out to your parents. It's enough."

"Mom didn't come out to talk to me," Toby said. He wasn't sure how she'd adjust. Usually she always deferred to Mike. "Was it hard for you, when you came out to your family?" Jared never talked much about his parents.

"My Mom I never knew. She split after having me. But my Dad...." Jared sighed. "I came to this garden when he passed away a few years ago. It was a comforting place to visit. I wasn't as brave as you were, Toby. I didn't exactly spell it out to him. But now I think he would have accepted it; he raised me on his own, despite being a truck driver, on the road a lot of the time. He could have dumped me like my Mom, but he made sure I had a home."

"Okay, if we don't deal with whoever"—Toby swallowed because now he knew who it had to be—"was behind the vandalism, we probably can't stay here too long, because we have to take care of the puppy."

Jared leaned close, playing with Toby's fingers as the wind breathed through the garden and the waterfall made soft splashing sounds. "Soon."

SAHARA BLUE leaned against Toby's car, waiting. Finally his patience was rewarded when a tall, blond and tanned woman with a ponytail appeared. He'd caught a look at her a couple of times before; Toby's former girlfriend, Anita.

She saw him and paused, tensing, obviously also recognizing him as a friend of Jared's.

Sahara pushed away from the car, smoky sunglasses hiding his expression.

"I don't want to speak to you," she said when he was closer. She clenched her hands around her briefcase, glaring at him.

"I just wanted to return this," he offered, handing her the scarf he'd found in the parking lot early that morning.

"That's not mine."

"I think it is." Sahara let it drop, indifferent. He read her, sizing her up with the experience of a man who has known combat, who has had to make instant decisions. "So I figured it out; you didn't do it because Jared's a man. You would have done it if he'd been a woman. It's just that Toby accepted the break-up too easily, and you'd expected him to stay under your thumb; it hurt your pride. You wanted to hurt Toby and you knew the best way to do that was by hurting someone he loved."

Anita shook her head. "He loved me."

"'Loved' as in the past, lady," Sahara said very gently. He looked up at the tall, shiny powerhouse condo building where she lived. "Nice place you have."

Anita's eyes widened.

"It would be a shame if what happened to Jared's home ever happened to yours," Sahara noted.

"THREE-THIRTY tomorrow," Jared said, writing it down on his old-fashioned hanging calendar with pictures of water lilies and Buddhas. "We should be able to get the pup his shots at the vet's."

Toby was unpacking pet supplies. The puppy jumped on his leg, clawing, but then a second later lost interest and began to chew on his sneaker.

He and Jared had been a couple of hours getting home and found Tina and Ellen had helped themselves to some wine and crackers and were feeling quite relaxed while on puppy duty.

"Why do I think I'm not ready to take care of a dog?" Toby asked.

"We'll walk him around the rough grass above the wharf after he eats something," Jared said. "Have some wine." Then he gestured through the glass of the new window. "There goes Sahara."

"He runs too much," Toby said.

"He's lonely," Jared noted. "He needs someone in his bed."

"Speaking of beds, what happens when puppy goes to sleep in his new dog bed?" Toby asked, coming under Jared's free arm as Jared worked with the organic dog food, blending a mix by hand. Toby was surprised he hadn't bought Albert something scented, like doggie incense. He'd be sure to tease Jared about his idea later.

"Then we'll find something to do in our own bed," Jared said, smiling at Toby.

SAHARA BLUE had reached a good pace, body on auto pilot as his mind roamed free. His muscles had a good burn going, and he liked the feel of the air pumping through his lungs, of how strong his arms and legs felt. He knew he could keep this pace up for another half hour before he'd have to ease down.

His face blurred past him in shop windows. He saw lingerie, leather belts and jackets, and some strange-shaped lamps in a lighting store that reminded him of one of the futuristic worlds imaginative Lotus sometimes wrote about.

Something ahead caught his eye. A dark figure running. The sound of shattering glass.

Heart pounding, Sahara dropped, checking out the gray outlines of buildings.

No. No, this wasn't his past. This was just some punk who broke a window.

Shaky, a little sick, Sahara regained his feet slowly. After a deep breath, he moved forward.

He had to make sure no one was hurt by the glass, maybe call it in to the cops. He fished out his BlackBerry and headed for the vandalized shop.

SETH was frozen by the stairs when a soft voice called out, "Are you all right in there?"

Shit! Whoever it was had to have eyes like a cat, to make him out where he was cringing in the shadows, sweating inside the dark confines of his dye supply shop. He waited, still afraid to move forward.

"Look, I can see you back there. I just called the cops." The figure raised a BlackBerry. "I'll stay out here until they come by. Just try not to be so scared, okay?"

The voice was strong, male, gentle, and protective. Seth was lured a little closer so he eased to the front of his store.

The man had his back turned now, his head down. He was wearing shorts and a T-shirt that clung to lean muscle and a high, perfect ass. His legs had sandy hairs and his running shoes were black pull-ons. As if feeling Seth's gaze, he looked up and familiar killer blue eyes stabbed into the shadows, looking into Seth.

It was Sahara Blue.

"It's you," Seth whispered with a feeling of strange inevitability, as if they had always been meant to meet, one way or another.

Chapter 24

A PET makes a house a home!

Jared smiled as he read the needlepoint pillow scrawled with cheesy sentimentality. Toby must have bought it on a tag sale hunt with Ellen. He was really getting into that lately in the month since they'd started living together, and he'd even taken up sometimes spending time looking at antiques. The pillow shouted to Jared that he wasn't alone anymore; he'd never have chosen it himself, but it was perfect for *their* home together.

Albert was snoring on their couch next to the new pillow, the microfiber coming in handy with a little puppy whose bladder was still catching up with the rest of him. The long body was sprawled out, his little legs up in the air.

Jared gave the pup a caress and then reached for his mandolin case, running a hand over it. Toby had bought him a new instrument shortly after he'd moved in. It was made by a man up near Jai in Mendocino. It played like a dream, and tonight was the first time Jared would sing at a club in a while. He took a deep breath, feeling the velvet weight of the bag in his pocket.

He set the security system Sahara Blue had customized for their home and locked the new door, which reflected the starlight. The merman and his sailor, looking an awful lot like Toby as he dragged Jared down into the depths.

Very appropriate. He couldn't imagine life now without a loving boyfriend. And his boyfriend actually being the guy he'd yearned for, thought he'd never have, was his Disney ending.

Tonight he hoped to show that to Toby.

At the club, Jared nodded to a few people he recognized. Some fellow musicians who knew he'd suffered the loss of his beloved instruments and had no doubt come to show their support were there, and at one table right at the front of the stage was Jai, who had flown down to see him. Sahara Blue was wiping the foam from his draft of beer from his lips, and Toby sat beside him, blond mussed hair, bright blue eyes shining.

Toby was staring up at Jared on the stage, his attention rapt, and it occurred to Jared that this wasn't anything new. His "best friend" had looked at him like that for years. He was glad fate had given them both a nudge in seeing that as unlikely as it had initially seemed, they could build a life.

Jared started off with some Vivaldi, taking the more classical tones with the bright running water sound of his mandolin. He switched to some medieval pieces, *cantiga 119,* relaxing into the warm-up, the first time he'd played in public for months. And finally, sweating under the bright focused light, he played a song he'd written for Toby.

Watching him, seeing him lean forward and his eyes widen, Jared knew his silent message had been received.

AS JARED tuned his instrument, Toby raised a brow at Sahara. "I haven't heard from Anita in a long time."

Sahara gave him a bland look in response. "Is that right?"

"You never did tell me what that errand was, the day you insisted on coming with me to see my stepfather."

"Nothing important." Sahara slouched back in his chair, looking as serene as one of Jared's Buddha statues.

"Hmmm." Toby saw Jai's eyes were sparkling, so he wasn't fooled by their taciturn friend. "So where's that new shy friend of yours, the one you've been spending all this time with lately?" Toby asked.

A shy look of his own moved over Sahara's features. "I'm working on him."

THEY left together after the show.

"Should we have left the others behind?" Toby asked back at the wharf parking lot. "You seemed in such a hurry to hustle me off." The last was said in a purring note, since Toby didn't need much convincing.

"I think that Jai and Sahara can entertain themselves," Jared said. "They can find their own men." He nuzzled Toby. "Seems like Sahara already has, since he's been hanging around Seth so much."

Toby laughed as Jared's nuzzle tickled him. With Jared's arm around him, he felt the same peace he'd always felt when they were friends. He looked up at the old, familiar building where Jared had guided them. They hadn't been back there since Jared's home was torn apart. Toby had figured maybe Jared needed some time. Plus they'd only just begun living together, and it wasn't an easy adjustment for two men who had never done that. And then there was Albert.

"Is it okay to leave pup?" he asked, feeling like a parent taking a night off.

"I asked Sahara if he and his new boyfriend could puppy-sit for us," Jared said. "I wanted time alone with you."

"Okay," Toby smiled, feeling shy himself. Just what were they going to do in that sexy, unforgettable space?

ONCE there, as if it were easy, choreographed, Toby removed his clothing as soon as they were in the room and the door was locked. It was a little drafty, but not too bad, and he walked to one of the windows and looked out at the harbor, at their floating home, its lights lit.

Jared came up behind him, simply holding him, his warm, clothed and bigger body a solid, reassuring weight against Toby's nudity. He slid his hands over Toby, caressing his chest, touching his nipples, his hands moving down the smooth lines with appreciation.

It was comfortable and erotic, like the slow wash of warm water against Toby's body, immersing into lovemaking until he hardened and Jared stroked his cock, every touch saying, *I love you, I love your body, and I love to touch you.*

After a moment, Jared pulled away, and Toby caught the sound of Jared's zipper, loud in the quiet of the space, and he heard the rustle as Jared removed his own clothing. Toby waited, hot and anticipating but also content.

Jared rewarded his patience by sliding slow hands down his back, and it felt so good that Toby's toes curled. He sighed, leaning into Jared's touch as he continued the caress until Toby was leaning against the brick wall siding by the window. "All right?" Jared asked softly.

"Oh yeah," Toby answered.

Lube and cool fingers probed; Toby tensed and relaxed, having learned how to accommodate his body to Jared's. And then he felt Jared's familiar thick cock, pushing in.

"Uhhhh." His head fell back against Jared's shoulder. Jared kissed the side of his neck and his hand reached up, nesting his fingers with Toby's as they moved together. Toby remembered imagining this scenario when they'd first come to this big empty space, but he'd never imagined it would be more than sex. It would be mating.

JARED was rubbing Toby's calf muscle since he'd gotten a charley horse out of the blue. Toby reached for a towel which Jared had brought with them for clean up, and he wiped his damp face while watching the careful attention Jared gave him as he cared for Toby's strained muscles.

"This is why I fell in love with you," Toby said. "Right from the beginning, you were always taking care of me. I'd never experienced that, and I wasn't raised to believe I should even like or invite it."

"You took pretty damn good care of me when I needed it," Jared said, as if shrugging off Toby's upbringing. He looked at Toby seriously. "No way I could have recovered so quickly from what happened to my home without you, Tobes."

"I couldn't leave you hurting," Toby said. He felt that way about all the patches in his life, that he wished he could mend them. Toby had met with his Mom once since he'd come out to his folks. She hadn't said much and had avoided the topic of Jared altogether, but she'd hugged him after they'd shared a coffee and Danish, and it had meant a lot. Maybe if Lorraine was finding her way, Mike might become more comfortable with time. Maybe Toby might have the chance to forge a new relationship with his parents as an adult.

"Toby, the other part of the evening is… I'd like to do something I'm not sure you're ready for. It's only been a month since you moved in," Jared said, looking nervous for the first time this evening.

Toby held his lover's eyes, watching him as he sat up, wiping the rosemary and olive oil cream from his hands he'd used to massage Toby's leg.

"Hey, we just had sex, and then I got a leg cramp right after I came," Toby said ruefully. "When I had the stomach flu right after I moved in, you took care of me and that wasn't fun."

"You were a sorry sight," Jared agreed, tenderness lighting his eyes. "But I loved taking care of you."

Jared had never nursed anyone through a flu or cold before, so he'd pulled out all the stops: homeopathy, special healing incense, rubbing Toby's shivering back with peppermint oil and then giving him the most tender blow jobs when Toby was feeling just a little bit better, and Toby had lain there, feeling cherished. It was one of his nicest memories of their first days together, when he'd thought being sick would just be a big drag for his partner.

"So what could be so bad you don't want to share it with me?" he asked.

"Not bad." Jared chewed his lip. "Just…." Then he shrugged and took out a velvet bag from his jeans, which were lying crumpled next to where they were reclining.

Toby blinked, suddenly having the feeling that whatever to come was significant in some way. He took a deep breath, bracing himself as Jared shook out two rings.

"Oh shit!"

Jared looked terrified. "You don't like them?"

"I—" Toby reached out and picked up one band, examining it more closely. It was silver and copper and gold with the shape of undulating mountain slopes and round diamonds hanging above like the moon and stars. It looked maybe like more of Tina's work, the artist who had made the door for their home. Immediately it made him feel good to hold the ring, as if it possessed some kind of legendary magic. "Jared."

Jared shoved back his hair, wide eyes questioning. "It's, um, a representation of Yatsugatake Mountain in Japan."

"It's beautiful," Toby said softly.

"Will you wear one and be mine?"

"Dork." Toby tugged Jared's face closer, so they were a breath apart. "I love the idea. Which one is mine?"

After a lingering kiss, Jared pulled away and slid Toby's band on his ring finger. He looked into Toby's eyes.

Holding Jared's gaze, heart thudding, Toby took the other ring and placed it on his partner's finger. "I love you," he said, wanting Jared to know, to feel it.

"There's a second part to my gift," Jared continued gravely. "I'd like to take you with me on my first trip to Japan. I would have bought tickets already but I wanted…. I'd like to plan it out with you. Look at websites and decide where we'd both like to go. In making a home with you, I've seen that it's kind of nice doing shit like that."

Toby swallowed. He'd always been a little nervous about traveling and had barely done any beyond his home state, but he'd always known they'd do this together. And now he could feel a little anticipation, like a small fire growing. Something told him he'd love this trip. "Okay," he agreed.

BACK at Jared's floating home—and also his now—Toby was happy to find Seth and Sahara still hanging out, both men drinking some Indian beer Seth had brought over. They'd been playing on Sahara's laptop, since originally they had somehow connected online.

Sahara immediately noticed the rings. "Geez, you guys." But he was smiling, his vivid blue eyes showing that he was happy for them. "So, I was thinking about going sailing on Saturday," Sahara continued, handing Jared and then Toby a beer from the case in the fridge. He gave his new boyfriend a pointed look. "Anyone feel like going with me?"

"I don't know. I'm still seasick from the last time," Seth complained, curling up on the sofa sleepily. "You insist on taking me out on the rubber thing and going far too fast and hard."

Sahara laughed, looking unrepentant. "I like fast. And hard."

And Seth blushed, but when Sahara netted his fingers with Seth's, he looked pleased.

Seeing that their puppy would need to be moved so they could all sit down, Toby picked him up and then leaned against Jared's legs, feeling Jared's hand tangled in his hair as he listened to Seth and Sahara decide on their next sailing adventure.

Jared was quiet, too, but soon he dropped down from his chair and pulled Toby into his arms so they were sitting together, their puppy in Toby's lap. Toby felt the peace he'd always experienced with Jared, in this sanctuary that was their home.

He'd found what he was looking for.

JAN IRVING has worked in all kinds of creative fields, from painting silk to making porcelain ceramics, to interior design, but writing was always her passion.

She feels you can't fully understand characters until you follow their journey through a story world. Many kinds of worlds interest her, fantasy, historical, science fiction, and suspense—but all have one thing in common, people finding a way to live together—in the most emotional and erotic fashion possible, of course!

Visit Jan's blog at http://jan-revealed.livejournal.com.

Also by JAN IRVING

Other stories of BDSM Romance
from DREAMSPINNER PRESS

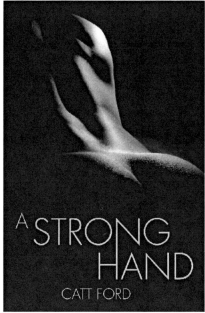
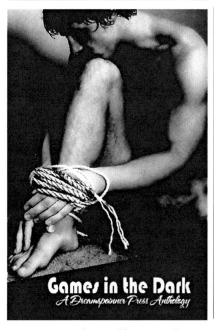

http://www.dreamspinnerpress.com

LaVergne, TN USA
12 October 2010
200540LV00004B/89/P